EBURY PRESS

THE GIRL WITH BROKEN DREAMS

Devashish Sardana is the author of the national bestseller *The Girl in the Glass Case*. After graduating from IIM-Ahmedabad, he has sharpened his storytelling skills as a brand builder in P&G and L'Oréal for over twelve years. Currently, he lives in Singapore with his wife and college sweetheart, Megha, and flits across the globe selling hope in a jar (beauty creams).

THE GIRL WITH

BROKEN DREAMS

DREAM AT YOUR OWN RISK

DEVASHISH SARDANA

EBURY
PRESS

An imprint of Penguin Random House

EBURY PRESS

USA | Canada | UK | Ireland | Australia
New Zealand | India | South Africa | China | Singapore

Ebury Press is part of the Penguin Random House group of companies
whose addresses can be found at global.penguinrandomhouse.com

Published by Penguin Random House India Pvt. Ltd
4th Floor, Capital Tower 1, MG Road,
Gurugram 122 002, Haryana, India

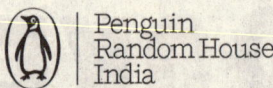

First published in Ebury Press by Penguin Random House India 2023

ISBN 9780143463726

Typeset in Adobe Caslon Pro by Manipal Technologies Limited, Manipal

Printed at Repro India Limited

www.penguin.co.in

This is a legitimate digitally printed version of the book and therefore might not
have certain extra finishing on the cover.

PROLOGUE

 Audio Journal of *THE DREAMCATCHER*
Audio File #1

This is a love story.

Ha! Sorry, I can't keep a straight face with that sweeping statement. Let me rephrase.

This *was* a love story. And then, it was more.

Have you read *The Fault in Our Stars* by John Green and cried into your pillow? Or watched its movie adaptation and wailed, with your mouth full of half-eaten popcorn? I have. Because, well, it was my story. Our story. Exactly like that book, but ours. Sonali's and mine. Two broken souls brought together by circumstance—the teensy inconvenience of cancer and the weensy nuisance of clinical depression. Two witless young adults trying hard not to scratch each other with the sharp edges of our splintered souls.

Don't worry. It's not a sad, romantic, coming-of-age young adult story. As I said, it *was* a love story.

And then, I killed Sonali.

1

Aamani unlocks the *Dream Box* with trembling hands.

It's a maroon jewellery box sheathed in soft, luxurious velvet with a golden clasp. The box is large enough to house the British monarchy's imperial crown. The only oddity—instead of a coveted brand name like *Tiffany* or *Tanishq*, embossed on the lid, in metallic gold and an elegant, italicized font, are the words: *Dream Box*.

A lightning bolt illuminates the night sky outside. The white light of the thunderbolt seeps in through the mullioned window of the hostel room, casting a dark, diamond-patterned shadow on the stone floor.

Aamani coughs, and coughs again. She pauses and inhales deeply, hauling broken chunks of air into her lungs.

She has been smitten by the *Dream Box*—covered in Christmas wrapping and a red velvet ribbon—since it arrived earlier in the day at the warden's office in North-Eastern Hill University (NEHU), Shillong, where she is pursuing a bachelor's degree in social sciences. The *Dream Box* is her going-away present from the Dreamcatcher. Months of planning, weeks of practice and 'the big night'—the Dreamcatcher's words, not hers—is finally here. For Aamani, it would be the night of good riddance. The last night.

Aamani lets go of the breath she was holding. She clenches and unclenches her fingers, unclasps the box and pulls it open.

Immediately, the woody, sensuous smell of musk tickles her nose. The muscles in her body relax; relief sweeps her away like she is a surfer riding a tidal wave. Such moments of pure, pain-free serenity are rare for her. She latches onto every puny bit of calm, knowing what comes next. She coughs and coughs again. Her lungs are on fire, as if a piece of them has been ripped apart, grabbed, jerked, and yanked out. Such moments of incessant, excruciating coughing are plenty. Moments she hopes to leave behind tonight. Aamani grabs the box and steadies herself. She pulls out a matchbox and a hot pink candle from the box, the source of the musky scent. She places the candle on the windowsill and lights it. Soon, her hostel room, which resembles a grubby, train-box prison cell, is engulfed in the overpowering aroma of musk, like a run-down spa trying to hide its rotting upholstery behind an overwhelming fragrance. Aamani doesn't mind. It smells much better than her sweat, which reeks of the cancer that is eating her from within.

Lung cancer. Stage II. Curable.

The doctor had said that she could expect to live for ten years or longer through a combination of surgery and chemotherapy. That was six years ago. She doesn't remember much else of what the doctor had said. Her father had gripped her hand and done most of the talking. Later at home, he had held her in a bear hug and whispered, 'We can beat this, Guddu!'—his voice cracking after each word. And she had pushed him away and retorted, 'Ha! Like you helped Mumma beat cancer?'

She isn't proud of what she had said. That day, in that moment, she was livid. Not at him, but *for* him. He is her favourite person. Her roly-poly 'Teddy Papa'— that's what she calls him. A kind, cheery man who sings for no reason, breaks into a dance for every small reason, whose eyes light up every time he sees her, a man who has spent every waking moment taking care of her since she was four and Mumma left with the Grim Reaper. Lung cancer. Same as hers.

Life has come to a full circle over six years since that dreadful diagnosis from the doctor. Years of chemotherapy and agonizing pain were followed by a few precious years of living cancer-free. And then, last month, the disease reared its ugly head again. Stage II, again. The Grim Reaper was back. This time for Teddy Papa's 'Guddu'. All that painstaking effort, all that unbearable suffering. For what?

Aamani looks down at the *Dream Box*. A teardrop falls and moistens the plush velvet of the box. She sniffles and wipes her eyes with the back of her hands. She nods. She is certain. The time has come. Both she and Teddy Papa can do without more suffering.

Aamani plucks the remaining items from the box: a set of wireless earphones that look like Apple AirPods but are squarish, a coin-sized stick-on device branded *Dreamo*, and a syringe with a needle that is thick and long enough to penetrate the tough skin of an elephant.

Aamani gulps. She is scared. Will it hurt? The Dreamcatcher had promised, 'It'll be over even before you feel the prick.' She trusts the Dreamcatcher.

Aamani deposits the contents of the box on the bed. She has one last thing to take care of before she sleeps. She takes out her mobile phone and calls her favourite person.

'Hello, Teddy Papa?' she says when her dad answers on the second ring.

'Haan Guddu, I was just thinking of calling you.'

Aamani closes her eyes and bobs her head twice. That's why she is calling now, lest papa calls later and interrupts her when she needs all her strength to let go.

She knows what comes next. The same three questions. Every. Single. Night.

'You had dinner, Guddu?'

'*Hanji*, papa.'

'Took medicines?'

'Hanji.'

'Did meditation?'

'Hmm . . .' she mutters.

'Good, good.' Papa seems satisfied. '*Achcha*, remember we have a chemo session in the evening tomorrow? I'll come to the college to pick you up.'

This is precisely why she lives in the hostel even though she belongs to the same city—Shillong—her city of birth, soon her final resting place. She loves her dad, but sometimes, just sometimes, all she needs is a wee bit of breathing space.

'I will . . .' Aamani coughs, and coughs again. 'I will come on my own, Teddy Papa. I'll meet you at the hospital.'

Silence. It seems papa is deciding whether to prod her.

'Okay. *Theek hai*, Guddu. As you wish.'

Silence.

'Teddy Papa . . .'

'Haan, Guddu?'

'I love you . . .' A lump grows in her throat. '. . . always remember that. Even when I'm not around.'

'Guddu, are you okay?' He pauses. 'I think you should come home tonight. I am coming to pick—'

'No, no, I'm okay. Just missing you. That's all.'

Silence.

Finally, papa exhales loudly over the phone. 'I'm missing you too, Guddu.' He pauses. '*Issi baat pe Lata Mangeshkar ji ka ek gaana yaad aa gaya* [I am reminded of a Lata Mangeshkar song in this moment].' His voice is bursting with happiness. Maybe, all a parent needs to hear is that their teenager still loves and misses them.

He starts to hum and sing. '*Lag jaaa gale [Let's embrace] . . .*'

'You and your songs!' Aamani interrupts him. 'I'm going to sleep, papa. Good night!'

Papa chuckles. 'Okay, okay. Good night, Guddu . . .' And he hums and sings the last verse of the song. '*. . . shayad, phir iss janam mein, mulakaat ho na ho—*'

Aamani disconnects the call and bursts into tears. It's the truth in Teddy Papa's parting words, the last verse of the song, '. . . *in this life, maybe we shall never meet again.*'

Thunder strikes. Rain drops, like tiny pebbles, start pelting at the window. Her entire body shudders as if urging her, begging her to stop. Stop now, before it's too late.

She shakes her head. *No!*

Aamani taps the Telegram app, a secure and encrypted chat service, on her phone. She opens her Secret Chats and taps the one right on top. The Dreamcatcher. And she calls him before she changes her mind.

A man with a gruff, heavy baritone answers the call. 'Aamani.'

She wheezes. Gulps a mouthful of air. Steadies her trembling hands. Massages her thumping chest.

She says, 'I'm ready to sleep.'

2

THE DAILY TIMES

NEW DELHI, FRIDAY, JULY 8, 2022

National Mental Health Crisis

FIVE TERMINALLY ILL DEPRESSED TEENS COMMIT SUICIDE

Aamani Sangma, eighteen, a first-year student of the North-Eastern Hill University (NEHU), Shillong, was found dead in her hostel room on Thursday morning. Aamani's father, Dilip Sangma, an IAS officer of the Meghalaya cadre, raised an alarm when his daughter failed to answer calls repeatedly. The university security found Aamani unresponsive in her bed after breaking down the locked door. She was later declared brought dead at Civil Hospital, Shillong. As per sources, Aamani had been battling lung cancer for six years and was recently diagnosed with clinical depression.

Aamani is the fifth terminally ill teenaged girl to have died by suicide in many months. All five deceased—the other four from Kolkata, Ranchi, Madurai, and Chandigarh—resorted to the same means to kill themselves: self-administering a large air bubble into the bloodstream from a gauge-7 needle, the largest manufactured in India. Suicide notes were found in all cases inside customized jewellery boxes embossed with the words 'Dream Box'. The victims held themselves responsible for their deaths in the suicide notes.

'It seems like a social media challenge gone wrong,' said Sub-Inspector Kudoi Thakur of Meghalaya Police. 'There are too many similarities to ignore in the five cases.' As the five suicides transcend state boundaries, he said, 'I don't know about the other cases. But, in the case of Aam-

9

ani Sangma, we must rule out murder first. The autopsy will be performed soon.' *The Daily Times* learned that in the previous four cases, the autopsies confirmed death by suicide and the cases were closed.

The suicide rate in India has increased by 13 per cent in 2021, as per the National Crime Records Bureau (NCRB). Unofficial sources claim that the number is much higher. It raises the important question of mental health in a country where youth have been battling unemployment, COVID-driven stress, and constant peer pressure on social media. Dr Niti Haldar, a clinical psychologist and the President of Doctors-ForSeva Foundation, was quoted as saying, 'The Central Government must address the rising mental health crisis among youth — asking a central agency like CBI to investigate the five identical suicides would be the right first step.'

The motives behind the mass suicides aren't clear yet. But it's clear that this is just the beginning.

3

Assistant Superintendent (ASP) Simone Singh flicks away beads of sweat streaming down her bald, squishy scalp, watching the clock on the Jeep's dashboard flip over to 10:10. She is now ten minutes late for her appointment with the therapist.

Simone had arrived five minutes before her scheduled appointment, but she has been sitting in the crumbling, Central Bureau of Investigation (CBI)-issued Jeep without air conditioning since. A dry, sultry breeze rushes in through the fully open window, smacking her sweat-speckled face. She detests the summers in Delhi. Even more, she detests the heat crawling up her back and the sweat seeping down her spine.

Simone is parked in front of a plush red-brick bungalow in Delhi's posh Lutyens Zone. The bungalow stands well back from the pavement behind lush jamun trees. Probably explains the sweetness in the searing breeze.

Her hands grip the steering wheel, knuckles white. Simone is thinking, wondering if she wants to keep her job with the Indian Police Service (IPS). Her boss, Superintendent of Police (SP) Vijesh Jaiswal, had given her a simple choice after the 'incident' last month: meet the CBI-appointed therapist or get suspended. Simone would have happily gotten suspended—it wouldn't be the first time anyway—rather than lie on a sofa and discuss her private affairs with a sham doctor, a stranger. But she knows it isn't a choice. It is a direct order from a superior. And she isn't one to break the chain of command. Orders ought to be followed. Period.

She pulls out her phone and flicks through her photos. Simone stops at a photo of her grandma, where she is beaming at the camera, waving a knife, about to blow out the candles on her eightieth birthday.

'You see what I have to do because of you, Grams,' she says aloud. 'You had one job. One. To stay . . . alive.' Her voice breaks.

Simone waits, hoping grandma would answer back, calling Simone '*bachchu*' again in her sing-song voice. Sigh. If only photos could talk.

Let's get this over with. Simone pockets the phone, puts on an N95 mask, tucks her police cap underneath her arm, and jumps out of the Jeep. She marches to the front gate of the bungalow.

A constable on sentry duty watches her approach, his gaze jammed on her shaved head. Her gleaming baldness has always invited glares. But she is used to the stares and the furtive glances. This is a choice. She had cut her locks two years ago when she had a run-in with the chief minister's son in Bhopal and was wrongfully suspended. She has shaved her head ever since. Initially, as an act of defiance, now as a proud battle scar.

The constable sees the IPS insignia on her shoulder flash and salutes her immediately. 'Good morning, madam ji!'

'What's the point of wearing a face mask that covers your mouth, but not your nose?' Simone admonishes the constable, whose face mask has conveniently slipped to his chin. The pandemic might have fizzled out, but good hygiene shouldn't. And neither should common sense.

The constable flashes a broad grin, his tobacco-stained teeth on full display. 'Sorry, sorry.' He hastily pulls up his mask, covering his hideous teeth. 'How are you, madam ji?'

Simone recoils. She doesn't have the patience for greetings or small talk. Simone has never understood why people do it. She comes to the point. 'I have an appointment with Dr Dia Sengupta.'

'Oh, minister sahab's daughter?'

Simone narrows her eyes. Granted that the bungalow belongs to one of the cabinet ministers. But how does being the daughter of that minister define a grown, accomplished woman's identity?

'No, I'm not here to meet the minister's daughter. I'm here to meet Dr Dia Sengupta, one of the leading therapists in Delhi,' Simone corrects him.

The constable scrunches his forehead, confused. 'Yes, madam ji. They are the same person. Same to same.' She wants to thump the constable on the head because they are not the same.

But it'll mean prolonging a conversation that she didn't want in the first place. Abruptly, she turns away from the constable and strides to the unbolted front gate.

'Wait, madam ji, you must sign the entry register,' he calls after her.

Simone stops. Like it or not, she believes that rules must always be followed unless they contradict her values and ethics. She sighs. Turns around. The constable runs to her with an open register and a pen. She scribbles briskly and hands back the register.

The constable squints at what Simone has written. 'Vijay Singh's daughter?' he reads aloud and looks up, confused. 'Who is Vijay Singh? Your father?'

'Yes.'

He chuckles. 'Madam ji, you had to write your name, not your father's name.'

Simone nods in agreement. 'As you said, they are the same person. Same to same, right?' Simone swivels on her feet and marches to the front gate without another word.

* * *

A woman is waiting for Simone at the main door of the bungalow. The constable at the front gate must have called and given a heads-up, thinks Simone.

'Hello, ma'am. I'm Radhika, assistant psychologist to Dr Dia Sengupta. Follow me, please,' she says in crisp English. A silver nose ring attracts attention to her gaunt face, textured with expensive, flawless cosmetics. Her long, flowing hair is coloured burgundy, matching her off-shoulder blouse and knee-length skirt.

Radhika ushers Simone into an immense foyer, as big as a fancy hotel lobby. But, unlike a hotel, they have stripped the house of all grandeur and opulence. It's a typical public servant's house in India. Grand but grey. Dated and jaded. Instead of a chandelier at the entrance, a light bulb dangles with a loose thread. Wrinkled cotton curtains cover the windows instead of embroidered tapestry. The wall paint bears scars and stains of years of neglect, reminiscent of the many families that have called it home.

'This way, ma'am.'

Radhika guides Simone into a room adjoining the foyer. Dr Dia Sengupta's office. The nameplate on the door says so. It's the perfect place for an office—inside the house—so the visitors feel welcome, but well away from the private quarters to avoid intrusion.

The vibe of this room is very different, though. It's cosy and colourful. And filled with natural sunshine. It's in stark contrast to the morbid dullness that met Simone in the foyer. More importantly, the air conditioning is on.

'I'll get you some water,' she says. 'Please take a seat. Dr Sengupta will be with you soon.'

Simone sits at the edge of a pale, three-seater sofa, hunched forward, like a cat in a cage, ready to flee when the cage is opened. The cushy sofa, covered with a crocheted blanket, faces a wooden armchair. There is no desk in between—it's meant for an open conversation between the therapist and the patient. *Patient? Yep, that's who I am. That's what it has come to.* Simone's heart beats a little faster.

She swallows, her mouth dry, dreading 'the talk' with the therapist. All her instincts tell her to run away.

Orders are orders.

'Bravo!' Dr Dia Sengupta enters the room with a flourish, beaming, the *pallu* of her turquoise chiffon saree flowing in her wake. 'It only took you fifteen minutes to come inside, Simone. You did it!' She extends a clenched fist to Simone, expecting a fist bump.

Simone rises from the sofa and joins her palms together. 'Namaste, Dr Sengupta,' she says. Fist-bumping might be better than a handshake, but she isn't touching another human being right after the worst pandemic in the modern world.

'Namaste! Namaste!' Dr Sengupta unfurls the fist and joins her hands in greeting, the smile never leaving her face. Her energy is infectious. Except it infects Simone with suspicion. Simone has always distrusted people who do cartwheels for no reason. She trusts actions, not words, or worse, fake enthusiasm.

Dr Sengupta slips into the wooden armchair and crosses her legs. Not a single pleat of her saree is out of place. She has tied her hair in a neat bun. She is in her late thirties but looks older, with streaks of silver hair around her ears. 'Sit, sit,' she gestures to Simone.

Simone nods and sits down, still hunched forward.

Radhika hurries into the room with a glass of water on a tray. She offers the glass to Simone and retraces her steps, closing the door behind her. Simone cannot help but wonder if Radhika is the assistant or the house help.

Dr Sengupta remains silent the entire time, her eyes curious behind her horn-rimmed glasses that match her saree, roving and assessing, as if Simone is a piece of art, complex and intricate, waiting to be deciphered and explained. Simone avoids eye-contact and sips refreshingly cold water, hoping, praying that Dr Sengupta breaks the silence.

They sit in silence for another minute.

Simone fidgets in her seat. It's becoming awkward. *Is Dr Sengupta waiting for me to say something?*

Simone sighs, breaks the silence. 'Dr Sengupta, I am—'

'Please call me Dia. Just Dia.' Dr Sengupta smiles, and her flawless, dusky skin gleams with her.

'Dia,' Simone tries again. 'My apologies for being late. I was—'

Dia waves her hand as if shooing away a pesky fly. 'No, no, Simone. I meant what I said. You came, that's a win. Most of my patients don't show up on the first day, especially if they have been mandated by their parents or superiors, or . . .' She pauses, and leans forward, her eyes unblinking. '. . . or the court.'

Simone looks away, guilty of where her actions have brought her.

'So, I mean it when I say congratulations for showing up, Simone. Well done!' Dia picks up a box of sweets from the side table and offers it to Simone, like a reward for a kindergarten kid for keeping her nose clean.

Simone shakes her head. 'No, thank you. No sugar for me.'

Dia nods and keeps away the box. 'So, what made you come today, Simone?'

'They ordered me to come here or lose my job.' Simone doesn't mince words.

'Is that the only reason?'

'Yes,' Simone says point-blank.

Dia bobs her head a few times and picks up a pen and a notebook from the side table. 'I hope you don't mind if I take notes while we chat.'

'Your office, your rules.' Simone fakes a broad grin, a churlish imitation of Dia's ever-present smile.

'Thank you,' says Dia. 'So, how are you feeling today, Simone?'

'Sweaty. Irritable. Dead inside.'

'What's making you irritable?'

'The heat outside. My boss. Your unwavering smile.'

Dia laughs out loud. A bit too loud. Fake.

'And why do you feel dead inside?'

'Because my grandma just died and . . .' Simone stops suddenly, realizing that she is falling right into the therapist's trap.

'And what Simone?'

'Nothing.'

Simone looks at her wristwatch. 'Can I go now? I came, so you can mark my attendance and I'll be on my way.'

Dia closes her notebook. She takes a deep, loud breath. 'Simone, that's not how it works.' She leans forward. 'Look, I'm trying to help you. I know it's painful losing a family member. It—'

'Not *a* family member. I lost *the* only family I had. And . . .' Simone gulps hard.

'And?' Dia prods her.

Simone shakes her head. She was forced to come here, but she can't be forced to talk.

'Go on Simone. I want to understand why it is so painful for you.'

'I. I . . .' Simone stutters.

Suddenly, Simone's phone rings. She takes it out of her pant pocket. She gets up from the sofa. 'Sorry, I need to take this. It's my boss.'

Simone doesn't wait for an answer. She makes a rushed exit from the room, the foyer, into the searing heat outside. She gathers herself, clears away the sobs choked in her throat, and answers the call.

'Jai Hind, sir,' she says.

'Jai Hind,' says SP Vijesh Jaiswal. 'I hope I didn't disturb your counselling session with the therapist.'

'No, you called at the right time, sir. We just finished.'

'Good, good.' He clears his throat. 'Listen, Simone. The CBI has been asked to investigate identical suicides in multiple states. Similar suicide notes, the same cause of death. It is being claimed that it could be a social media challenge gone wrong or mass murders. *The Daily Times* published an article on it yesterday. Read it. The latest suicide happened in Shillong two days ago. I want you to take charge, head over to Shillong and start the investigation.'

Simone inhales deeply. This is too close to home for comfort. She clenches and unclenches her fingers.

'I know this might be uncomfortable, Simone, given the past couple of months. But I'm trusting you. I think this can be therapeutic and keep you focused on the job.'

'Yes . . . yes, sir.' Simone stutters. 'Thank you for trusting me, sir. I'll be on the next flight to Shillong.'

'Good, good. I'm assigning Inspector Pereira to the case. He will assist you.'

Simone rolls her eyes. *Not Pereira.* Inspector Lucas Pereira was chirpy, chatty, charming and competent. Simone only cared for one of those traits. Lucas was a rank below Simone—an inspector—but Simone, the same age as Lucas, was on the IPS fast track—a luxury given to a select few officers who had cleared the mother of all exams in India, the Union Public Service Commission (UPSC). Only 0.1 per cent of a million Indians, who appeared for the exam, cleared it each year. Simone was one of them. Lucas wasn't. But Lucas had something that Simone did not—unfettered optimism. It'd be a matter of time before she burst his bubble of positivity with her sharp, pointed cynicism.

'All the best, Simone. Keep me posted.' SP Jaiswal disconnects before Simone can voice concerns about Inspector Pereira.

Simone exhales out loud. Surprisingly, she feels lighter, as if she tripped and fell, but on a trampoline. Maybe SP Jaiswal is right. Maybe this is the therapy she needs. A fresh case. A fresh start. A chance to clean up the bloody mess of the last two months. She needs this case. She needs it to prove she is capable, more to herself than others.

Simone turns on her heels and strides back to the Jeep, a spring in her step and without another thought for Dr Dia Sengupta. She came, marked her attendance and indulged in a forced, awkward chat—that should be good enough for the CBI brass. And the court.

4

Audio Journal of *THE DREAMCATCHER*

Audio File #2

Sonali and I met at a party, a Zoom party, organized by the good folks at the Dream Cancer Foundation during peak COVID. Don't ask me why they named a cancer support group 'Dream'. Cancer is no dream. There is no frolicking in fluffy white clouds where you chase candy-pooping unicorns riding mammoth bunnies shouting 'Yee-haw!' Cancer is one of those dreams where you fall into a black, unending abyss, and the only way to stop the endless suffering is to shoot yourself in the head. Good luck finding a gun. It's a dream, sure. But there is another word for it. The right word: nightmare. The name Nightmare Cancer

Foundation would have been more apt if you ask me.

Anyway. It was a party. And every Zoom party must have a theme, right? So, there I was in the theme, 'Festive Pyjamas', in my most vivid grey T-shirt, dusty grey slacks and matching underwear (I was hoping to get lucky). Well, that's what you get when a teenager is forced to follow the free will of their parents: a rebellion.

And there she was. Sonali. One among the thirty-odd blank-faced teenagers on a Zoom screen. Dull as a dying star. Pale, like a squeezed nimboo. Chemotherapy does that to the brightest of us. Not that Sonali was the brightest. Far from it. But she had a spark in her eyes. A twinkle. Easy to miss. And just so that I did not have to debate with my mind later, I took screenshots when she introduced herself to the group. Lots of screenshots. Memories for later viewing. Proof for later inspection. Art, for my collection.

I sent her a heart emoji on the group chat after she introduced herself. I am forward that way. Think it, say it. She replied with a 'Thanks!'

Thanks? Seriously! That's what you get when you pour your heart out to someone? Maybe I should have sent three heart emojis? Less than three is too formal. More than three looks childish.

Bottom line: she rejected my heart the first time. I accepted her 'thanks', determined to try harder.

I don't remember much else about the rest of the party. I was either glued to Sonali's pinned screen during the call or scouring social media for any signs of her. I found more than signs. The moron had, still has, a public profile for every voyeur on the net. And before you get ideas, I wasn't being a peeping tom. I was in love! I followed her on Insta, Snapchat and Twitter. I liked every photo, every reel, every video she had ever posted on Insta. You see, I don't do things half-heartedly.

I thought for a few minutes—ok, ten minutes probably—and sent her a private message on Insta: 'Hi! Good connecting with you during the Zoom party. Looked like you had a tough chemo session today. Hang in there!' That should have been a stalker alert, a clear red flag. Luckily for me, she ignored the red flags and responded with, 'Hi! Thank you for the support during the group meet', and a black heart emoji.

A heart! She sent me a heart! Okay, it was a black heart, but OH-MY-GOD, a dazzling, beating, cancer-infested heart!

And I realized. People like supportive people. And nothing brings people closer together than shared suffering.

5

Simone dashes to the bathroom with a zip-lock in hand. She gathers her toiletries with gusto, places them one-by-one—neatly and deftly—in the zip-lock, and seals it. She checks her watch.

'Fuck!' she murmurs. The flight to Shillong is in two hours and she isn't packed yet.

Simone rushes back to the bedroom and dumps the zip-lock in the space chalked out for toiletries in the suitcase flung open on the bed. Her Samsonite suitcase looks like a bento-box tray—every item divvied and separated according to size and utility. Marie Kondo, the queen of tidiness and her idol, would be proud, she muses.

For the first time in months, a spark of excitement is bursting through her heart. A glimmer of hope, of light at the end of a long, dark tunnel of despair. These new cases—of similar suicides by cancer patients—are a lifeline, a rescue boat when Simone was flailing in the deep sea, struggling to keep her head above water. They might be what they are—suicides—but, as a police officer, the search for *why* they did it gives her purpose. Something to look

25

forward to, some way to be useful. She is scared to stay alone, without work, with her dark thoughts, afraid she might do it again.

Simone is zipping the suitcase when the doorbell rings.

She isn't expecting anyone. And she'll be damned if it turns out to be a cosmetics salesman.

Simone strides to the front door, wheeling the suitcase with her. She deposits it next to the door and flings the door open.

An overweight, voluptuous woman in her late thirties, wearing a khaki police uniform, stands akimbo at the door, a soft smile caressing her lips.

'Zoya!' Simone exclaims.

She rushes to embrace the woman, wraps arms around her girth and squeezes her tight. Deputy Superintendent of Police (DSP) Zoya Bharucha is the only friend she has. And now, since grandma died, the only family, the only well-wisher.

Their relationship wasn't always so rosy. Simone and Zoya had partnered on the last case, back when Simone was posted with the Bhopal Police. Simone had hated her niceness and Zoya had hated her guts. But after a rocky beginning, they had learned to collaborate and nabbed the Doll Maker, India's most notorious serial killer, in the case dubbed as *The Girl in the Glass Case* by the press.

Then, Simone was transferred to the CBI Headquarters in New Delhi, and they lost touch.

'It's so good to see you!' says Zoya.

'It *so* is!' whispers Simone, a catch in her throat. She embraces Zoya more tightly, squishing into her soft flab.

And without warning, tears well up in her eyes. Her heart is suddenly full, and it comes pouring out. Her body shakes and she sniffles. She hasn't cried like this since grandma died, but now, in Zoya's arms, Simone couldn't bottle the sorrow any longer.

Zoya rubs Simone's back. 'It's ok. Let it out.'

'Grams passed away,' Simone mumbles, words tumbling out incoherently while she cries, her mouth half-open.

'I heard. I'm so sorry, Simone.' Zoya pats her back. 'I called. Many times. But you didn't answer because . . .' Zoya pauses before saying, 'I also heard something else.'

Simone pulls away from Zoya's embrace. She knows what Zoya is alluding to. She doesn't want to talk about it. Simone wipes away tears with the cuffs of her shirt. She ignores the question. Instead, she says, 'Come in, come in.'

Simone ushers Zoya inside the apartment.

'What brings you to Delhi?' asks Simone.

Zoya eyes her intently. It wasn't lost on her that Simone changed the topic. Zoya says, 'A family function. Thought I'd come and give you a surprise visit. But I can't stay for long. Sunny starts panicking if I'm away for long.'

Zoya is a single mom; Sunny is her only son. Simone had saved Sunny after he was abducted and nearly murdered by the Doll Maker when they worked together on their last case.

Simone brightens up. 'How's Sunny?'

Zoya shrugs her shoulders. 'Some days are good. Most days, not so much. The panic attacks haven't stopped since . . .'

Simone nods. She understands how abduction and a near-death experience can wreck the mental health of a five-year-old.

They stand in silence, nobody sure what to say next.

'Were you going somewhere?' Zoya breaks the silence, nodding towards the suitcase.

'Shit! I totally forgot. I have a flight to catch in less than two hours.'

'Good for you! The Simone I knew never took a vacation,' Zoya chuckles.

'I still don't,' says Simone, puffing her chest, proudly. 'I'm back on active duty. Going to Shillong on a fresh case.'

'Umm . . . is this a good idea?'

Simone crosses her arms. 'What do you mean?'

'I mean, considering the events of the last couple of months, isn't it too soon?'

'Sure, grandma died, but I'm learning to deal with it.'

Zoya bites her lower lip. 'I wasn't talking about grandma. I was talking about the other thing . . . the thing you don't want to talk about.'

Simone stiffens. She is cornered. Nowhere to go. Suddenly, she doesn't want Zoya here anymore. The longer she stays, the more difficult it becomes for Simone to keep the broken pieces of her life together.

'I'm running late. I must really leave for the airport now,' says Simone, rubbing her sweaty palms together.

'Okay. Let me drop you to the airport. It'll give us a chance to catch up.'

Simone is taken aback. She knows why Zoya is offering a ride. Zoya wants a lowdown on why Simone did the *thing*. Simone herself doesn't know why she did it. It was a spur-of-the-moment thing. It happened. Why does everyone want to talk about it? Get over it already!

'It's okay. I'll take my Jeep and park it in the long-term car park.'

Zoya watches her closely. 'I insist,' she says.

Silence. Simone is speechless.

'Fine,' she says, defeated. 'But on one condition. We are not talking about it.'

'About what, Simone?'

Simone stays mum.

Zoya walks over and holds Simone by the shoulders. 'I just want to know if you are fine.'

'I'm fine. More than fine.' Simone's voice cracks. Tears well up again. *Why am I getting so emotional about it?*

Zoya tightens her grip. 'Are you?'

Simone hangs her head, unable to control the tears streaming down her cheeks. 'No,' she says, shaking her head. 'Of course, I'm not fine.' The truth tumbling out, finally. 'I tried to commit suicide, Zoya. How can I be fine?'

6

'Look! Isn't it beautiful?' Lucas squeaks in glee, the deep dimples forming and un-forming on his cheeks, his curly hair flopping all over, his forehead jammed to the tiny window of the aeroplane, pointing to the vast, lush, undulating hills surrounding Shillong. Despite being in his late twenties, Lucas is like a kid aboard a plane for the first time. His energy is palpable, his enthusiasm infectious.

Lucas has been chatting non-stop for two hours on the flight from Delhi to Shillong. Simone has learned more about Lucas during the flight than she knows about her parents. Lucas was born in Goa, half-Portuguese, the eldest of three siblings, but his mom—a primary school teacher—relocated to Delhi, her hometown, when Lucas's father died prematurely of a brain aneurysm. The family of four moved into a one-bedroom rented house in Punjabi Bagh. Lucas was chubby in middle school—yes, it's hard to imagine—he had told Simone, seeing his lithe, athletic figure now. 'Fat pig'—that's what other kids had called him.

A bullying incident left him scarred for life. It was 18 August 2004, Wednesday. Apparently, he has a photographic memory. He remembers running across the schoolyard in his cotton-white underwear, snorting like a pig—his seniors in high school had forced him to—while his classmates jeered at him. He still gets nightmares about that incident. Subsequently, he lost weight, insecurities and bullies. It's curious how your perceived beauty is directly proportional to the number of friends you have in school, Lucas noted.

He is single, never married and engaged once. The girl left him standing at the Church altar—exactly like it happens in American soap operas, he had mused. He is best friends with the girl, now since she is divorced. No, he is not interested in her 'that way' anymore. Friends, just friends, he had clarified. Lucas showed Simone the photos of when he was born, his first day at school wearing knickerbockers and stockings, a cheery photo of him winning a consolation prize at a drawing competition, his first girlfriend, his first dog, a Cavoodle who died of old age, his second dog, also a Cavoodle named Po after the Kung Fu Panda . . . *Phew!* The first thing Simone wants when they land is an aspirin.

Now, squashed in the middle seat, Simone steals a glance at the hills, drawing closer and closer as the plane descends. Nausea hits her, and she looks away. Simone swallows hard and sits upright. Her stomach churns. She hasn't eaten anything since the morning. And the surprise visit from Zoya left her more spent than spirited. She grips the two armrests, crushing the soft edges inside her palms. Her knuckles turn white, her lips pale. Her heart pounds, her ears buzz and sweat bursts through the pores on her back. She closes her eyes and starts counting in reverse—a little trick grandma had taught her to overcome the one fear that has plagued her since she and grandma got stuck mid-air inside a cable car once: the fear of heights. Breathe, Simone bachchu, breathe, grandma's calm voice rings in her ears.

'Hundred, ninety-nine, ninety-eight . . .' Simone murmurs.

'Are you okay, Simone?' asks Lucas. 'Do you need water?'

Simone doesn't answer. Her focus is on breathing and staying alive. Funny how it was only last month that she wanted to stop living.

'I'm fine,' Simone says, finally, her eyes still rammed shut.

Slowly, the wave of nausea passes. Her heart eases a little, her chest heaves a little less. Simone opens her eyes, looking dead straight at the grimy backside of the seat in front. She doesn't want to make the mistake of looking outside the window again while the plane descends.

Simone senses the piercing eyes of Lucas on her, probing, seeking and questioning if Simone is fine.

'Stop staring at me. I said I'm fine,' Simone hisses.

'You want to hold my hand?' asks Lucas, unperturbed.

'What?'

'Hold my hand.' Lucas offers her an open hand. 'My sister is afraid of flying as well. Holding hands helps her during take-off and landing.'

'I don't have a fear of flying. I have a fear of heights.' Simone grips the armrest more tightly.

'Yeah, yeah. Same, same.' Lucas smiles. 'Give me your hand. Trust me.'

Simone has never been a touchy-feely person. She doesn't like human touch, doesn't understand the need for human intimacy and doesn't see the point of getting close to someone, especially a stranger.

'Come on. I won't bite you. I promise.'

Begrudgingly, she peels away her left hand from the armrest, wipes the sweaty palm on her trousers and offers it.

Lucas tangles his fingers into Simone's and squeezes them a little. Lucas's hand is stiff, but somehow, feels warm. 'You'll be fine, Simone. Trust me. You'll be fine.'

Simone takes a deep breath. She isn't certain if Lucas is talking about her fear of heights or her failed suicide attempt. Though the truth is told, holding Lucas's hand now, this human touch makes her heart feel slightly full.

* * *

'Did we get consent from the state government yet?' There is urgency in Simone's voice, her tone teeming with annoyance.

Lucas shakes his head, his ear pressed to the phone, waiting for a response from the office of the advocate general of Meghalaya.

Simone and Lucas have been stranded at the airport Arrivals Lounge for two hours now. They want to directly visit the crime scene at NEHU, Shillong. The only issue: the CBI still hasn't received official consent from the

Meghalaya Government to investigate the case of Aamani Sangma. In March 2022, Meghalaya became the ninth Indian state to revoke general consent to the CBI. The central agency can no longer pick, choose and intervene in any police case it likes—a step to mitigate political interference by the Central Government in the state's matters using CBI as a pawn. No consent, no interference from CBI.

Her boss had promised Simone that the notification of consent will be in place by the time they land in Shillong. Simone looks at her digital watch now. 16:40. Twenty minutes before the office of the Advocate General shuts shop for the day.

Fools! Such tardiness should be unacceptable—but had come to be expected—in a bureaucracy that was so burdened with a legacy of laziness. A legacy built and strengthened by movies. And the movies were right. Mostly.

'*Arey, aur kitna time? Jaldi kijiye,* please [How much more time? Please rush],' Lucas says on the phone, nudging and prodding the advocate general's secretary on the other end.

He is too nice, thinks Simone. Niceties can't pierce through the tough, thick skin of people used to being kicked around. They need a thump on the head to get things done. Simple.

Lucas disconnects the call before Simone has a chance to snatch away the phone and give a piece of her mind to the secretary herself.

'What happened?' asks Simone.

'The secretary said to call back again tomorrow. They are working on it.'

'Tomorrow? It's a simple notification letter.'

'I know.'

'They have been working on it the whole day. They don't need an entire day to draft the letter!'

'I know.'

'We don't have the budget to stay another day, Lucas. And we are wasting time.'

'I know.'

'Can you please stop saying *I know*?' Simone raises her voice, her eyes glued on Lucas, unblinking.

Silence.

She closes her eyes and exhales. There is no point bashing the messenger to death. There is a problem to solve. Lucas or his niceness is not the problem.

Simone paces. She isn't ready to accept defeat, go home and come back again tomorrow. She stops. She remembers something she read in *The Daily Times* article. A tiny detail. A simple mention. But it could be the key that unlocks this impasse. She pulls up her phone and opens the article. *There it is!* The tiny detail: the profession of the victim's father, Dilip Sangma—a senior IAS officer with the Meghalaya cadre.

In a bureaucracy marred by tardiness, nothing moves things faster than a *danda* from an IAS officer.

* * *

The chilly evening breeze rushes in through the window and smacks Simone in the face. She likes cold. Her favourite weather; her favourite emotion.

IAS Dilip Sangma had responded as any bereaved father would. The CBI, the nation's most prominent investigation agency, wanted to dig into his daughter's suicide to figure out the motive, the cause. There was a possibility that it wasn't a suicide at all. Maybe a murder. That *maybe* was enough to convince him. The simple, harsh truth is that any father, any parent, would rather blame a killer for murdering their kid than fathom the heart-rending, intentional choice of suicide. Suicide leaves parents at a crossroads, confused—who is to blame? All Simone had to do was give Sangma hope that Aamani hadn't chosen to end her life.

IAS Sangma had taken all of ten minutes to get them notification of consent from the state government. In return, he had requested all investigation updates. Daily updates—he had stressed it. You scratch my back; I scratch yours. Simone wasn't too enthused. But she had agreed to the deal.

Now, they are hurtling across National Highway 6—a spunky new asphalt road that cuts through the rocky terrain—on their way to NEHU, Shillong. The local CBI office sent a Jeep with a driver as a courtesy. The Jeep is as old as the highway is new, sputtering and wheezing on the smooth, near-empty road.

Simone is engrossed in the police reports from the five known suicides so far. Lucas is engrossed in the view from the car—the luscious green hills that breeze past them.

'Such nice weather na?' Lucas muses. 'Perfect for chai.' He turns and faces Simone. 'We should have had chai at the airport.'

Lucas waits for Simone to say something, but when she doesn't, he turns away. And just as quickly, he swivels his head again. 'It's like you are cramming for an exam, Simone. We read the police reports on the flight. And then at the airport. Each report is crystal clear. Death by suicide. Nothing new will pop up, no matter how many times you read the same pages.'

'I don't have a photographic memory like you do, Lucas. Lesser mortals like me must do with cramming.'

'You want me to quiz you?' says Lucas with a twinkle in his eye.

'Nope.'

'Come on! It'll be fun.'

Simone stops reading. Looks up. 'Fine.' She tries to hand him the reports.

'I don't need them.' He smiles and knocks on his temple with his index finger. 'It's all in here.'

Simone smiles back. 'Alright, Mr Cocky. Shoot.'

'What were the dimensions of the *Dream Boxes* received by the victims?'

'The dimensions?'

Lucas nods, biting his lower lip.

'Who cares?' Simone throws up her arms in mock protest. 'It was a box. What it housed is more important than its size, no?'

'It was on page 1 of all five reports. You must remember after all that cramming, no?' The dimples dig deep into Lucas's cheeks as he grins. 'They were all 18x18x15 inches.'

Simone crosses her arms. She prides herself on her attention to detail. She is used to knowing everything about her cases, no matter how trivial the question. 'Ask me another one,' she says. 'But no useless trivia.'

Lucas mulls it over for a second. 'One out of the five reports mentioned an unusual smell at the scene of a crime. Which one?'

'Ranchi!' exults Simone, like a contestant on a game show. 'It was woody, caustic, and . . .' Simone looks at the ceiling of the car, trying to remember. '. . . and musky.'

'Correct,' says Lucas. 'Next question—which victim did not lock the room from inside when she committed suicide?'

The question stumps Simone. She doesn't remember reading this bit in any of the reports. How did she miss it?

'Do you give up?'

'No!' Simone shakes her head vigorously. 'Give me a minute.'

But Simone is none the wiser even after a minute. 'Yeah, I give up.'

'None!' laughs Lucas. 'It was a trick question. They'd all locked the doors from the inside. All five cases were identical.'

Simone glares at him.

'Not bad, Simone,' he says. 'You got one out of three. Congratulations! You barely pass with 33 per cent marks.'

Her nostrils flare; her forehead throbs. She shoots daggers at Lucas with her eyes. She wants to get back at him, poke him, provoke him. Simone has always been a bad loser.

'Are you making fun of the victims?'

Lucas stops laughing. 'Sorry, I didn't mean it that way.'

'Tell me, Lucas. Have you ever tried to commit suicide?'

His face contorts. It's like the question jabbed him in the face.

'Let's say you wanted to commit suicide. What would you do?'

Lucas thinks—the lines on his forehead creased in an awkward grimace. 'I guess . . . I guess I'll first decide how to kill myself. Painless and swift. And then just get on with it.' He pauses. 'Ah!' he says as he suddenly remembers something. 'I'll leave behind letters—one each for my mom, siblings, best friend, and Po, my dog.'

Simone smiles. 'Well, I didn't have anyone to write to when I attempted suicide.'

Simone stops herself. *What is happening to me?* It stumps her how easily the truth flowed off her lips. One meeting with Zoya, one emotional outpour and suddenly she is announcing her suicide attempt to the whole world?

She notices that the driver in front shifts in his seat, as if uncomfortable with the direction the conversation has suddenly veered towards. Or, maybe, he is simply leaning back to hear more clearly. Curiosity.

Simone focuses again on the point she was making. 'Would you dress up for the suicide?' she asks.

Lucas's face is ashen. Clearly, he was not expecting this line of questioning. '. . . maybe.' He waits for a beat before asking. 'Did you . . . did you dress up?' His voice is low and soft, almost apologetic.

Simone swallows hard. She broached the topic. There is no going back now. 'I didn't dress up. I just went for it,' she says, trying hard to sound nonchalant as if recounting a boring day at the office.

She peers at Lucas. 'Last question—would you lock your door?'

Lucas thinks about it. 'I'm conflicted. I want to lock the door, but I don't want to make it hard for my family to find me. Don't want them to break down any doors.'

He is too nice, thinks Simone. Even on a hypothetical question, he is thinking about others first.

Simone says, 'You know, I bolted the front door. Locked the bathroom door. And jammed a standing vanity cabinet against the bathroom door from the inside. Every minute mattered. Every second counted. So, I made it as difficult as I could for someone to find me.'

Silence. Lucas looks down at his feet, uncomfortable. The driver in front sits upright, his shoulders tense.

'The point I'm trying to make is that every suicide has a different nuance. And the more suicide victims you compare, the more differences you'll find,' She pauses. 'But all five cases are the same. Identical. We found a jewellery box inscribed with the words *Dream Box* in all cases. The victims had the same squarish earphones in their ears, the same 'Dreamo' stick-on device on their foreheads. They all plunged a gauge-7 needle meant for horses into their necks. And all of them had their phones completely scrubbed, all data wiped off when they were found dead.'

'Yes, so something connects all these cases,' says Lucas.

'Not something. Someone. Someone sent them the box, and the earphones, and the stick-on device, and the gauge-7 needle.' Simone straightens in her seat. 'I think . . .' Simone looks ahead. 'I think someone murdered them.'

7

**Audio Journal of *THE DREAMCATCHER*
Audio File #3**

I would describe myself as a spiked pebble stuck in your shoe—annoying sometimes but excruciating on most days. Sonali burnished my spikes, calmed me down, and gave me purpose. Before you get any ideas, mind you, she was no angel herself. How do I describe Sonali without sounding presumptuous?

Sandpaper!

Yep, Sonali was like sandpaper. Smooth on one side; abrasive, bloody hurtful on the other. It was exciting, to be honest—not knowing what personality of hers you'd meet on which day. As Forrest Gump would say, my Sonali was like a box of chocolates. You never knew which one you were going to get.

Sometimes, I wondered if the cancer had turned her into a sore bitch. I was even callous enough to say it to her face once after she berated me endlessly for lack of colour in my wardrobe. Grey, grey, grey! Who doesn't wear any other colour? Me! So, I told her that cancer had turned her into a bitch. What can I do? I don't have a stopper in my mouth. It was during a WhatsApp video call a month after we first met. Just the two of us sparring and bickering, getting to know each other. She told me without a pause, 'Cancer is no excuse for who I am. This is me! Accept or move on, bitch!' Yep, she had called *me* a bitch. I have never wanted anyone as badly as I wanted her at that moment.

And we stopped talking and went back to watching the movie together. That was our pact. If we fought, we wouldn't hang up the call. We'd watch a movie together—she on her laptop, me on mine while straying on the phone so we could hear each other gasp, scream or cry. We did that a lot. Movie marathons. Because we fought a lot. Mostly, she'd pick the movie. Mostly, it'd be a horror movie. Mostly, I did the gasping and screaming and crying, while she laughed out loud at the timid scaredy-cat that is me. And puff! The fight would be over, and we'd go back to chatting and bickering and scratching.

Horror movies—that's what I miss the most about Sonali. *The Ring* was her favourite, *The Ring Two* is mine—it's so remarkably bad that it's good. No wonder then that my favourite movie inspired me to plunge an air bubble into Sonali's bloodstream with a syringe. That's how I killed her.

Movies: they entertain, they educate—if you are paying attention—even the bad ones.

8

A local police officer, unshaven and dressed in police khaki, salutes Simone as she steps out of the Jeep in front of the Girl's Hostel, NEHU, Shillong.

'Jai Hind, ma'am!'

'Jai Hind! Are you Sub-Inspector Thakur?'

The man smiles, revealing two missing incisors on the top, which make him look like a withered old man, betraying his age of early thirties. 'Yes, ma'am. Myself Kudoi Thakur. Please call me Kudoi. Welcome to Shillong!' His cheery voice reminds Simone of a concierge welcoming guests at a beach resort.

Simone had requested Shillong Police for assistance from the lead officer on Aamani's case. The local police had considered it an open and shut case of suicide. A sub-inspector was appointed, no investigation was done and the case was closed in two days flat. Simone is certain it took them two days because that's how long the paperwork would have taken, not the investigation.

'What happened to your front teeth, Kudoi?' asks Simone.

Lucas shakes his head at Simone's directness.

Kudoi lolls his head back and laughs, revealing the naked gums where his front teeth would have been. 'I used to be a boxer. Under-16 state champion. Got into a street fight after drinking a bit too much. Didn't know that the other guy was an under-19 national champion. I lost two teeth and my dignity. Stopped boxing and drinking, and joined the police force when I turned of age. Arrested that bugger the first opportunity I got. My first arrest.' His chest puffed a little with the pride of his deed.

'So, you were an underage drunk and joined the police to exact revenge?' Simone summarizes.

Kudoi stops smiling. He clears his throat, but no words tumble out.

Before it gets more awkward, Lucas intervenes. 'Thank you for coming to assist us, Sub-Inspector Thakur. Can you show us the crime scene—the victim's hostel room?'

Kudoi clears his throat again. 'Certainly.' The broad grin is back. 'This way, please.'

The Girl's Hostel is a three-storied brick building, constructed in a U-shape, painted white with baby pink panelling, next to the paved and aptly named Hostel Road. There are no walls around the hostel. Only a barbed wire strung around and across thin, lush green trees: an open invitation for any intruder—or lover from the Boy's Hostel—to skulk in without notice.

Simone makes a mental note. If this was a murder, the killer could have easily waltzed in and out of the hostel. It still doesn't answer how the killer waltzed out of the hostel room that was locked from the inside. One step at a time, thinks Simone.

'We've closed the case, but we haven't handed back the room to the university yet,' says Kudoi as he leads them to the second floor of the building through a dingy staircase. Residents—studying or gossiping or loitering—give them furtive glances before going about their business. It seems they have become accustomed to the police parading inside the hostel for the last week.

Aamani's room is in the middle of the floor. 'The premium wing: one person per room,' Kudoi explains. He distributes white rubber gloves and shoe covers to both. Simone nods in appreciation. The sanctity of a crime scene is paramount, but mostly disregarded once a case is closed.

'Did you speak to her neighbours or friends?' Simone asks, pulling on a pair of rubber gloves.

'Yes, spoke to the girls living in both the adjacent rooms. They didn't hear a thing. Both heard about Aamani only when they came back from classes the next day and saw the police hovering like flies on this dump,' says Kudoi as he removes the crime scene tape in front of the rickety wooden door and unlocks it. He flings the door open. 'Welcome!'

Simone enters the narrow train-box like room first, followed by Lucas. A musky, stale odour assaults her nose.

'What's that smell?' asks Lucas, sniffing twice. 'Was the body kept here for long?'

'Few hours, maybe,' says Kudoi. 'The coroner took it away as soon as the forensics were done collecting evidence.

We thought the smell is a combination of her deodorant and cancer.'

Simone rolls her eyes. *Idiots!* Simone has been around dead bodies long enough to know that they don't putrefy for at least three to five days after death, even for cancer patients. And they certainly don't have a musky undertone. 'This isn't the rotten smell of a dead body. Or cancer. This is sweet, woody and musky. Did you find deodorant in the room?'

Kudoi evades Simone's stare, realizing his mistake. 'No.' He shakes his head. 'Oh!' he says, suddenly remembering something. 'We found a perfume bottle, though. Channel.'

'Channel?'

'Yes, the expensive French brand. Channel number five.'

Simone and Lucas exchange glances.

'It's called *Chanel* No. 5, my friend,' says Lucas, the dimples forming intermittently on his cheeks.

'Yes, yes. Channel,' he says coyly.

'But isn't Chanel No. 5 a complex perfume of floral and fruity notes? It's not musky,' says Lucas. 'I remember reading it in a magazine,' he turns to Simone and explains.

Simone has no clue about perfumes and the notes they strike. But she is getting more irritable by the second from the odour that has impregnated the confined space. 'Let's open the window and let some fresh air in, shall we?' she says.

Simone takes a few steps to the single translucent window at the back of the room. It's bolted. She sniffs. The musky smell is stronger here. The base of the windowsill catches her eye. She bends down and sees the remains of candle wax tacked together—grubby and pink. She sniffs again. Her face contorts. She has found the source of the smell.

She straightens herself. 'Kudoi, please get a forensic down here. I want to know what was in this candle that makes it so oppressive days after it has burnt away.'

'But . . .' Kudoi hesitates. '. . . how is it related to the case, ma'am? Maybe the dead girl was using it as incense. Or as a room freshener.'

'We don't know. But we must cover all bases, Kudoi.'

For Simone, it was the first rule of a police investigation: don't assume. Assumptions are the termites that gnaw and hollow out an investigation from within. In this instance, though, she remembers that the report from Ranchi Police—about the third girl who had allegedly committed suicide—mentioned a strange musky odour in the room. Lucas had even quizzed her about it during the car ride here. She had disregarded it as a trivial detail. Until now. One is randomness. Two is coincidental. And Simone doesn't believe in coincidences. After all, coincidences are nothing but assumptions. And nothing was often everything in forensics.

'Lucas,' says Simone. 'Call the local police who were investigating the other four cases. Ask them about the musky smell. And the candle. If they are unsure, get them to visit the crime scenes again and search for any remains of a melted candle.'

Lucas nods.

Simone keeps staring at him, unblinking.

'You mean now?' asks Lucas.

'Of course. When else?'

Lucas nods fervently, takes out his phone and scurries out of the room.

Simone turns her attention back to the room. But, after ten minutes of searching the tiny room, she is none the wiser.

'I'm done here, Kudoi,' she says. 'Let's visit the pathologist who performed the autopsy. I want to know why he thought it was suicide and not murder.'

9

Simone and Lucas follow Sub-Inspector Kudoi into the two-storied building of the Forensic Science Laboratory Meghalaya. The facility looks like a shipping container from the outside—rectangular and scarce, run-down and ramshackle. Kudoi tells them that this is the 'new' building. All forensic work in the state was previously done from two rented houses adjoining the 'new' building.

They enter the reception, register in the entry docket, and walk up to the second floor that houses the Chemical Division for Examination of Drugs and Narcotics in the left wing and the Biology Division for Examination of Dead Bodies in the right wing. The corridor is dingy and dark, despite the sun scorching the pavement outside. Kudoi leads them to the end of the corridor and stops in front of a door with the nameplate: Dr Paul Lyngdoh.

'You may go in. Dr Lyngdoh is expecting you,' says Kudoi.

Simone knocks on the rickety door, twice.

'Come in!' says a gruff voice from inside.

Simone enters. Lucas follows.

Dr Lyngdoh removes his thick, black reading glasses and stands up. He is frail and tall—the same height as Simone—and on the other side of fifty. 'Welcome. Please come in,' he softens his voice but still sounds hoarse, forced like he has a sore throat.

Simone touches the edge of her face mask, afraid to remove it. She was down with COVID—delta variant, last year. Two long, excruciating weeks that she doesn't want to live again.

Dr Lyngdoh notices Simone's obvious worry. 'I neither have sore throat nor COVID. Just my natural, sweet voice.' He forces a laugh. 'It's a birth deformity in the larynx. You may remove your masks.'

Lucas removes his mask. Simone doesn't.

'As you wish,' Dr Lyngdoh smiles.

The office is small, square with shelves lining the walls, replete with folders and dockets of every conceivable colour. It appears more like a mini library of dossiers than a medical examiner's office.

Dr Lyngdoh sits hunched, his elbows on the desk. 'Please take a seat.'

Simone and Lucas sit opposite him on the two wiry chairs for visitors.

'How can I help you?'

'Can you tell us about the autopsy results of Aamani Sangma?'

Dr Lyngdoh pushes a plastic folder towards Simone. He has been briefed. He is prepared. 'It's all in here,' he says. 'Aamani Sangma died of cardiac arrest due to an air embolism that she introduced into her bloodstream with a gauge-7 needle. We found only her fingerprints on the syringe. One puncture wound on the neck. Right into the jugular.'

'Any—'

Simone tries to say something, but Dr Lyngdoh raises his hand. 'Let me finish speaking before you ask questions,' he says like a veteran professor. 'We found no external wounds on her body. No sign of violence, no other fingerprint on her body. However, we found small traces of a dissociative drug in her bloodstream—ketamine.'

Simone wants to ask about the drug but keeps mum, for now.

Dr Lyngdoh eyes her and says, 'Dissociative drugs are a type of hallucinogen. They distort your mind and senses. Makes you detached from your surroundings. In small traces, you let go of your inhibitions. Ketamine is an FDA-approved drug that is used in medical settings for sedation, anaesthesia and treatment of depression. As you can imagine, it's highly addictive, hence, highly controlled.' Dr Lyngdoh pauses. 'We found traces of the drug in her nostrils, so we can be sure it was inhaled.'

'We found remains of a burned candle in Aamani's hostel room today. It might be the source,' Simone offers.

'It might,' Dr Lyngdoh gives a nonchalant shrug. 'Any questions?'

'Are you sure that it was suicide?' asks Simone.

'I'm quite certain,' he says. 'All evidence suggests that Aamani Sangma did this to herself.'

'What about the *Dream Box*?' asks Lucas.

'What about it?'

'Someone sent her the box, right?'

'She might have ordered it herself,' rebuts Dr Lyngdoh. 'And even if someone was helping Aamani, they didn't kill her. Her room was locked from the inside. And again, I must stress the fact that the final act—the act of killing— was performed by Aamani alone. Hence, suicide. Case closed.'

Simone shakes her head. 'Do you know how many girls have committed suicide in exactly the same manner in the last five months?'

'I know. Five. I read the same news article that you did,' he says.

Simone leans forward. 'Someone is behind this. Even if they are not pulling the trigger, they are providing the gun to these innocent, susceptible girls to take their lives. At best, they are an accomplice. Worst, murderers. Either way, we'll catch them.'

Dr Lyngdoh steeples his fingers. 'That's your job, officer. My job was to tell you how Aamani Sangma died. And I did.'

There is no point in stretching this meeting further. Simone pushes back the chair and stands up. 'I think we are done here. Thank you for your time, Dr Lyngdoh.'

He nods. Doesn't get up from his chair.

Simone marches out of the room, Lucas trails.

Kudoi is leaning against the wall, engrossed in his phone when they step out of the room. 'How did it go?' he asks.

'Intense. Is he always this stuck up?' Lucas asks.

'Always.' Kudoi chuckles. He peers at Simone. 'By the way, I got the information you had asked for—the sender's address on the Dream Box received by Aamani.'

Simone shakes her head. Kudoi had termed it a suicide and closed the case without performing a basic investigation. It looked like a suicide, so it must be suicide. Case closed.

'And?' Lucas asks.

Kudoi taps a few times on his phone and narrates the address. The place is in Chandigarh. It seems familiar. She has seen it before, somewhere. *Where?*

'Shit,' says Lucas. 'It's the address of the fourth victim.'

'Are you sure?' Simone blurts out before recollecting that Lucas has a photographic memory. One of the many trivial facts he'd told Simone during the two-hour flight.

Lucas grins. 'Challenge accepted.' He opens one of the files in his hand, about the Chandigarh case. The address of the fourth victim is on the first page of the FIR. He gives the file to Simone, a proud smirk plastered on his face.

'Can you tell us the address again, Kudoi?' says Simone.

Kudoi does. Both addresses match.

'So, the fourth victim sent the box to the fifth victim?' asks Kudoi.

Simone and Lucas nod in unison.

'It's intentional, part of the modus operandi of whoever is killing them.'

Lucas gasps. 'I think I know how to find the killer.'

'How?'

'I have a theory. But I need the sender's address on the box received by each victim.'

Lucas spends the next half hour obtaining the information from the local police. It confirms their finding. Each victim received the package from the previous victim, like a going-away present, from one to the next, forming a chain, a connection, like dominoes, one toppling after another.

'I think we have found the killer's address,' says Lucas.

'But that's clearly a setup, a misdirection,' says Simone.

'Yes, but what about the first victim, the very first suicide that started the domino effect?'

'What about it?'

'I think the sender's address on the *Dream Box* meant for the first victim is the killer's address.'

10

Audio Journal of *THE DREAMCATCHER*
Audio File #4

I'm the Dreamcatcher. I'm a druggie. I admit it. Why hide it? Why be guilty? Do you feel guilty when you have chocolate? Or when you have long, back-breaking sex? No, of course not. You do it for pleasure. Plain. Simple. Same with drugs. It's like sex, but better . . . because it lasts longer. Now, granted that I have an excuse: cancer. But do you hear me giving excuses for drugs? No. I do it. I do it for pleasure.

But do you know what's better than taking drugs? Taking drugs with your lover. The highs are higher, the lows are not that dire. Oh, it rhymes! Maybe I should write that down, write soul-searching poetry, sing heart-rending ghazals and solve life's puzzles. Oh, that rhymes too! Umm, maybe not. Sorry, I'm recording this while I'm high—major missing for Sonali today. Yes, yes, I killed her. That doesn't mean I can't miss her. Oh, that rhymes too! I'm on a roll, baby!

Crash!

. . .

. . .

Oops, sorry, I broke into a dance and dropped the voice recorder. Umm, where was I?

Yes, Sonali. The ache of my heart, the pain in my ass. She wanted to try it all—all kinds of psychedelic, mind-numbing drugs. Do you know how difficult it is to source drugs in India? Well, let me tell you—not at all! So, we made a list—a bucket list of drugs to try. And every night for a month, over our nightly Zoom calls—remember, this was during COVID restrictions—we ticked off the list, tried the drug of the day together. For thirty days straight, thirty different drugs. Cheers! Ah, the sweetest period of our relationship. And at the end of thirty days, we chose the winner: ketamine, hands down. No pain, no depression, only ecstasy . . . just for a while, but totally worth it.

We snorted it on our first night together, in each other's arms, our legs intertwined, naked. A piece of advice, my friend. Don't combine sex with drugs. You'll be sore, but you won't remember how.

11

Simone is eager, tapping her fingers on the steering wheel as she drives the CBI-issued Jeep. Lucas is fidgety, twisting and turning the turquoise bracelet —a *Feroza Patthar*— he wears on his right hand. The bracelet is a gift from his mother, meant to ward off evil spirits. She told him it's inspired by her favourite Bollywood actor, Salman Khan, who wears an identical bracelet. Lucas isn't a fan of the actor, but his mother is. He has never taken off the bracelet since she tied it around his wrist.

Lucas and Simone are back in Delhi, en route to the DDA Flats in Pocket 2, Dwarka Sector-9—the sender's address for the box received by the first victim. It's their first big break in the case. Lucas is excited. Somehow, he is certain that it's the killer's address. The first case is usually a trigger for serial killers, usually personal. It's likely the killer sent the *Dream Box* from his own address. Even if not, the killer is connected to this address somehow. All other addresses were chosen intentionally, carefully, to show a domino effect. Why else would he choose this address for his first victim? There must be a reason. They will find out soon.

Simone swerves the Jeep into the parking lot of the housing complex and brings it to a halt.

'Handcuffs?' she asks.

'I have them,' says Lucas.

'Let's go.'

They jump out of the vehicle and climb the worn stone stairs to the third floor.

Lucas checks the house number, nods to Simone, and rings the doorbell. He unclasps the holster of his service revolver. He is prepared in case they need to make an arrest.

A middle-aged woman, probably in her forties, answers the door. She is shrouded in black, a grim expression on her face. Deep, puffy, dark circles underneath her eyes suggest she hasn't slept in days.

'Hanji?' says the woman, her voice low, lifeless.

Simone says, 'We are from the CBI, investigating multiple cases of teenaged suicides. We'd like to talk to Sonali Anand.'

The deep wrinkles on the woman's face twist and contort. A sob escapes her dry lips, and she starts weeping. 'You people . . . have come now . . . after six months,' she says in-between sobs.

'Yes, can we speak to Sonali?' Simone presses.

'You are investigating the case and you don't even know!' the woman raises her voice.

'Know what?'

'Dead! Sonali is dead.'

* * *

Simone and Lucas sit across from the grief-stricken woman in her living room. Her loud sobs have given way to silent weeping.

'I told the police, but they didn't believe me,' says Mrs Anand, Sonali's mother. 'Sonali would never commit suicide, I told them. She was a headstrong girl, fearless and independent. She wasn't a coward who'd resort to suicide.'

Simone clears her throat, stays quiet. Unlike popular belief, suicide isn't synonymous with cowardice. Suicide requires every bit of the human spirit to end something so precious. Life. It's easier for the headstrong. Ask me, thinks Simone.

'Yes, she was depressed. But which cancer patient isn't?' Mrs Anand pauses as fresh tears stream down her pallid, saggy cheeks.

Simone gives her a moment before asking, 'I understand you've told this to the police before, but can you tell us how Sonali died?'

'Murdered. She was murdered.' Mrs Anand pauses, lets the words settle. 'Sonali was alone in the house for a couple of hours. I had gone to the temple next door for the evening *aarti* and *satsang*. Sonali's father was away at work. When I returned, I tried going into her room to give her *prasad*, but she had locked it from inside. I called out to her. There was no response. Something bad had happened, and I knew it right away. I called the ambulance. I thought Sonali might have fainted from fatigue. It had happened before. But I didn't understand why she'd lock the door when we had categorically agreed that she must never lock it. Ever. I have always respected her privacy. But a medical emergency can arise anytime with a cancer patient. So, we had agreed that she could shut the door, but not lock it.'

Mrs Anand sniffles before continuing, 'I rushed to our neighbour's house next door.' She lowers her voice conspiratorially as if sharing a secret. 'The husband lost his job recently and stays at home.' Then, in her normal voice, she says, 'I shouted, rang their doorbell. He helped break down the door. And there she was, my Sonali, on the bed, dead, as if she had died in her sleep.'

Mrs Anand stops, stares at the ceiling, lost in her thoughts.

Simone and Lucas steal a glance.

'How did she die?' Lucas urges her to continue.

Mrs Anand closes her eyes, as if the memory is hard, too painful to recall. 'The police say she plunged a syringe full of air into her own neck.'

Simone draws in a deep breath. *How did this case get missed?* Now there are six. At least. And this is the earliest case based on the timeline. Maybe there are more. She makes a mental note to double- and triple-check reported suicides across the country.

'Did you or the police find any box in her room?' asks Lucas.

'Box?'

'Umm, like a big jewellery box with words *Dream Box* stencilled on it?'

'*Dream Box*? No, there was no box.'

'Anything else the police found?'

Mrs Anand sighs. 'They found drugs in Sonali's room during the search and in her body during the autopsy.' She averts her eyes, as if ashamed.

'Did you know about the drugs?'

She nods. 'I knew. I was mad the first time I found out about it. But she told me the drugs helped her with the pain and the depression.' She looks Simone dead straight in the eyes. 'My daughter was terminally ill. I didn't want to fight her. I was happy if she was happy.' She pauses. 'I also know where the drugs came from. Her murderer.'

There is complete and utter silence.

'I told the police about her. Noor Shah. She was Sonali's best friend. When I pressed Sonali, she confessed Noor supplied her with the drugs. I told the police about Noor. I told them that Noor has something to do with Sonali's murder. But they gave her a clean chit, called it a suicide, and closed the case.'

Lucas asks, 'When you found Sonali, was she wearing any earphones or some stick-on device on her forehead?'

'Yes! How did you know?' Mrs Anand sits up straight. 'That was the other thing I told the police, but they didn't listen.'

'What?'

'Noor sent the earphones and that stick-on device to Sonali. Sonali told me herself when the package had arrived. I'm telling you, officers—Noor is responsible for my daughter's death.'

12

Noor unlocks the *Dream Box*, her hands steady. Her calm demeanour surprises her, considering what she is about to do.

Crisp notes of musk tickle her nose as she opens the maroon jewellery box sheathed in soft, luxurious velvet. She plucks out a baby pink candle from the box and lights it. Like the Dreamcatcher wanted it. She sniffs the aroma, her mind twirling, the muscles in her shoulders relaxing, as if she has snorted cocaine. She knows the feeling. The high. She'd felt it the first time she had tried magic mushrooms. Then again, with black tar heroin. And then ecstasy. And then meth. All psychedelic, mind-bending drugs. The musky scent of the candle seeping into her brain is similar. But faster, stronger. It's pulling her up, propelling her to a euphoric state. She felt like the weight of a dream—feathery, almost vapour-like. The best part: she's pain-free. The crumbling, cancer-ridden bones in her limbs don't ache anymore. Maybe it's just her mind playing games. But who cares?

Noor pulls out her iPhone 14 Pro and turns on her favourite song, *Lover*, by Diljit Dosanjh. Nothing better to pepper the mood than with a peppy song. She ramps up the volume to the maximum. Not that she's disturbing anybody, except maybe the neighbours. But who cares? It's just her, alone in the chic, lavish studio apartment that her parents bought for her. Noor sways with the beats, her eyes closed, her mind free, her arms wobbling wildly as a satin blouse hung on a clothesline on a windy day. She sings along. '. . . baby, baby. *Tera ni main, tera ni main, lover* [baby, I am not your lover] . . .'

One minute. Two minutes. And as suddenly as she had started, she stops dancing. She huffs, exhausted. The pain courses through her legs, hot like burgeoning lava. There is only so much a drug can do. Cancer triumphs, always.

Noor clutches the *Dream Box* between her arm and bosom, her phone in the other hand—still belting out the song—and staggers to the bed. She deposits the *Dream Box* on the bedside table and free-falls on the bed, the memory foam of the mattress absorbing her feeble mass. It's a canopy bed made of expensive mahogany wood with four elongated posts at each corner, draped in chiffon curtains resembling the feathers of a flamingo. The bed is out of fashion with its colonial-style frame, but it radiates sophistication in her cosy apartment. Her prim mother designed the interiors. It is the least that could be expected from a celebrity interior designer who works only with Bollywood wives and socialites. Who cares if a mother caters to rich clients in Mumbai when her daughter is fighting for her life in Delhi?

Well, it's a slight exaggeration.

One, Noor is dying, but slowly. The bone cancer is localized to her limbs. The doctors caught it early. Her five-year survival rate is 86 per cent; probably more because she is still young.

Two, Noor moved out of her parents' bungalow in Malabar Hill—the most affluent neighbourhood in Mumbai—of her own volition when she cracked the Indian Institute of Technology Joint Entrance Examination (IIT-JEE). She had the option to enrol at IIT Bombay and be closer to home, but IIT Delhi seemed a far more glittering gem. Not because of the city, or the engineering stream her rank could afford, but solely because she wanted to be away from her parents. Period. Well, they had been away all her life while the house help raised her. She was just returning the favour. For years, she only met her parents at the dinner table, bathed and combed and dressed by the house help, presented and showcased, as if the maid's salary depended on Noor's evening presentation. Every. Fucking. Day. Weekends included.

Three, Noor didn't bother to tell her parents about the cancer till she almost died during an emergency surgery due to a complication and the hospital called the first of kin. Her mother. The woman left her rich clients and rushed to Delhi with the house help in tow. Once Noor was discharged from the hospital, mommy dear went back to Mumbai, leaving Noor in the care of the maid. The next day, Noor gave the maid a few years' salary and fired her. The maid cried and declined the money, but Noor insisted. She is stubborn that way, a trait she has inherited from her master: her father. Speaking of whom, daddy dear hasn't visited her in Delhi even once. Though his money keeps visiting her bank account every month.

Noor sighs. There comes a point when stopping the train permanently is safer than a head-on collision. For Noor, she has reached that point tonight. It is time for a full stop.

Noor pushes herself up from the bed. 'Fuck, fuck, fuck!' she groans from the effort. And the pain. She once fractured her arm from turning abruptly while sleeping. It still hurts when she tosses and twists in bed on sleepless nights, which, if she hasn't pumped in enough painkillers, are most nights.

She taps the screen on her phone and pulls up her Secret Chats on the Telegram app. Dreamcatcher—the words shimmer right at the top.

She checks her watch. It's time to make the call and bring the train of her life to a screeching halt. A full stop.

13

'Any luck with the phones?' Simone asks Lucas, her eyes on the road ahead, jammed with traffic.

Lucas shakes his head. 'IT couldn't retrieve any data from the victims' phones. Wiped clean.'

'How about the call logs? The victims had earphones in their ears. They were listening to something. Or someone.'

'I spoke to the investigating officers in all the cases. All of them had checked the call log because of the earphones. The last calls were to or from family, friends or telemarketing companies. Everything checks out.'

'Everything?' Simone snorts. 'I don't trust them. Ask them to check it again. All of them termed it a suicide and closed the cases within a week. That's stellar or sloppy.' She peels her eyes away from the road and glances at Lucas. 'Knowing the sheer stress and volume of cases our local police forces handle, my bet would be on sloppy.'

Lucas smiles. 'You don't trust anyone, do you?'

'In God I trust; everyone else must bring data,' Simone muses.

'William Edwards Deming,' says Lucas.

'Sorry, what?'

'What you said. You quoted Deming, an American professor and statistician.'

'You have quite a memory, don't you?' Simone pushes the accelerator as the traffic eases in front of her.

Lucas shrugs his shoulders. 'It was helpful when I was a kid winning quiz competitions. Now, my brain is filled with crappy trivia that you can google, anyway.'

'You never know when your memory will help.'

They ride for the next ten minutes in silence.

'We're here,' says Simone, as she pulls the Jeep to a stop at the entrance of Tata Primanti, a posh gated community in Sector 72, Gurugram.

Simone flashes her badge to the security guard and gives him Noor's address. The guard gives her directions to the apartment block without her asking. Simone pulls into the massive compound and finds the right block in no time.

'How do you want to play this?' Lucas asks Simone.

'Tough. We come on hard.'

'She's just a kid, Simone.'

'She's nineteen. She's an adult.' Simone reminds Lucas. 'If she is hiding something, I want her to crack and spill the beans.'

Lucas nods and runs his hand through his hair. There is something pleasant about his shagginess. Simone has to resist the temptation to arrange his hair for him.

They get out of the Jeep. The elevator takes them to the twentieth floor. They step out into the lavish, enclosed corridor with a single apartment, the penthouse.

Simone rings the doorbell.

They wait. When no one answers, Simone knocks on the door and rings the bell again.

No answer.

'She doesn't seem to be home,' says Lucas. 'She's a student at IIT Delhi, right? Do you think she's at college right now?'

Simone presses the bell again. Maybe this cold call wasn't such a good idea, after all, she thinks. They should have called ahead. Now they are wasting time.

Lucas sniffs. 'Do you smell that?' he says.

Simone sniffs twice. A faint woody, musky odour tickles her nostrils. *Ketamine!* She goes down on her knees, bends her head and sniffs closer to the flat slit between the door and the floor. The smell is much stronger here. It's wafting up. *Shit!*

Simone springs back up and bangs on the door. 'Noor! It's the police. Open up!'

No response.

'We need to break open this door,' says Simone, her tone urgent.

Lucas steps back, braces himself, and lunges at the door, thrusting his entire body weight on the massive hardwood frame. The door doesn't move an inch.

'Fuck!' Lucas grabs his shoulder and winces in pain.

'Don't be an idiot, Lucas. This isn't a Bollywood movie. Doors don't fall apart like mounds of sand.'

Lucas massages his shoulder. 'I'll run down and get help. Or a hammer.' He gets into the elevator and is gone the next moment.

Simone paces in front of the door, panicking, dreading what she might find on the other side. *There must be something I can do.*

Suddenly, she remembers. Simone had learned Taekwondo for extra credit during IPS training. The instructor had taught them the basics of kicking down a door. Simone takes a deep breath and lines up the heel of her heavy police boot against the side of the door where the lock is mounted. She front-kicks her right heel into the lock, her left foot firmly on the ground. The door shivers. She kicks it again. And again. Simone is panting and sweating profusely after two minutes. Her foot hurts after three minutes. Her back hurts after four minutes. She is breathless, wheezing. And, finally, after five minutes of incessant, repeated kicks, the door lock splinters away.

Simone bends down, hands on knees, trying to catch her breath. Her instincts tell her she doesn't have time. She must hurry. No time to rest.

Simone lunges into the apartment. The house, a duplex, is filled with smoke and a strong, unbearable aroma of burned ketamine. Simone rushes to every room on the ground floor of the duplex. She finds no one.

Did I panic about nothing? A wave of relief takes root in her heart. No one is at home. *But then who is burning ketamine?*

Simone strides to the first floor, climbing two stairs at a time.

She peeks inside the first room next to the landing. It's a study room. It's empty.

She rushes on and peeks inside the second room. It's the master bedroom; massive, opulent, colonial. It's filled with smoke from half-burnt candles, the flames still dancing on the two bedside tables. There, lying on the bed, in a thin white tunic, is a feeble, malnourished girl. She appears to be asleep. Or dead.

'Noor?' Simone yells.

No answer.

And then Simone sees the signs. Noor has odd, rectangular-shaped earphones in her ears. A coin-sized device is stuck in the middle of her forehead. And a syringe lies on the ground, right below Noor's hand, which is dangling from the edge of the bed.

Simone bends down. She sees a puncture wound on Noor's neck. Blood has clotted around the puncture. *Shit!*

Simone checks her pulse. Noor is still breathing. For now.

14

An attempted suicide fails; a victim has survived. They rush Noor to Medanta, the Medicity Hospital in Gurugram, where the doctors revive her just in time. She's out of danger now. They inform her parents, who fly down from Mumbai.

The hospital calls Simone to inform her that Noor has regained consciousness. The police can question her now. There are questions to be answered. There are reasons to be questioned. Noor, Simone hopes, will unravel the mystery tonight. If they are lucky, the case could even be closed soon. Done, dusted, forgotten.

Simone brings the police Jeep to a sudden stop in the parking lot of Medanta. Simone pulls on her mask and jumps out of the Jeep, feeling the soft caress of the warm night breeze on her head. Lucas gets down the passenger side door and follows her.

The hospital facade is built like a fortress: stony, grey and majestic. The stained building fades in the twilight, casting long, dark shadows in the open parking lot.

Simone and Lucas march to the front entrance. A flood of white, piercing light welcomes them into the building.

The caustic smell of antiseptic cleaner overpowers the nostrils.

Simone stops in her tracks. She doesn't want to be here. She wants to run away—far, far away—and never return. Her heart throbs faster, filled with dread. She clenches and unclenches her fingers. Agonizing memories come racing back—memories of rushing grandma to the hospital emergency—of clutching grandma's lifeless feet and bawling like a child, memories of waking up in a hospital bed herself, alive, when all she wanted was to be with her grandma. Dead. She cannot be here. She cannot spend another moment in a hospital. Just cannot.

'Simone?' Lucas touches her shoulder.

Simone jumps in surprise.

'Are you okay? You are wheezing.'

'No . . .' Simone gulps. 'Yes, yes, I'm fine.' She gathers composure and controls the wheezing sounds she didn't even realize she was making.

Lucas narrows his eyes, clearly in doubt. But he doesn't push it. Instead, he says, 'I'll ask for the room number at the reception. You stay here.'

Simone nods and looks away. She doesn't want Lucas to see the tears that have welled up in her eyes. Something inside her plummets, like an untethered lift hurtling down a shaft. *Why does it still hurt so much?*

'Control, Simone. Control.' She sniffles, blinks away the tears.

This isn't good. She is relapsing, falling into the black abyss of depression. Again. Simone closes her eyes and hangs her head as it dawns on her: *I need help. I need help now.*

'Simone?'

Simone sucks in the air, looks up at Lucas. 'Got the room number?' she asks hurriedly.

Lucas pauses, stares at her, weighing his thoughts, as if unsure of what to say. 'Umm . . . yes. Second floor.'

'Let's go.' Simone strides to the staircase, not even waiting for the room number, afraid Lucas would rip open old bandages with a simple question: *are you okay?* Simone doesn't know how to answer that question anymore. Or, maybe, she doesn't want to . . . because answering it would mean admitting the truth that she's tried so hard to hide.

They don't have to try hard to find Noor's room. It's the only room with a police constable stationed outside. Standard protocol. Simone knows the drill. She was here a month ago. For now, Noor Shah is both the victim and the assailant. Attempt to suicide is a punishable offence under the Indian Penal Code (IPC). However, the Mental Healthcare Act decriminalized it in 2017, presuming severe mental stress leads one to commit suicide. It is now for the police to prove if Noor attempted suicide because of mental stress or some ulterior motive, based on which she either gets psychiatric help or one year in prison.

'Jai Hind, madam ji,' the constable salutes Simone.

'Jai Hi—' Simone stops mid-sentence as loud voices from inside the room interrupt them. 'What's the commotion?' Simone asks the constable.

The constable clicks his tongue. 'Nothing, madam ji. Family drama. The parents just arrived from Mumbai to see the victim. Apparently, she doesn't get along with the parents.'

Lucas snorts. 'Which teenager gets along with their parents? Trust me, I have a teenaged brother who is fully equipped with rolling eyes, deep sighs, and sarcastic comments—what's not to like about teens?' he shakes his head and chuckles.

A loud, incessant scream bursts from inside the room.

Simone rushes past the constable and dashes into the room.

It's a private room with a comfortable single bed and an attached bath. No frills. Clinical, cream, clean. Noor is sitting upright in bed and screaming hoarsely. The mother, dressed in a heavy silk saree and heavier gold jewellery, is sitting on a chair beside the bed, yawning, as if bored from the melodrama. The father, a heavy-set man in a navy-blue three-piece suit, is standing at the foot of the bed, his arms crossed, his forehead creased.

'Get out! Get out of here!' Noor shouts. She turns to the constable who's entered behind Simone, 'I don't want to see them. Get them the fuck out of here!'

Simone turns to Noor's parents. 'You need to leave. Now.'

'With pleasure,' says the father and storms out.

Deep sobs replace Noor's incessant screams. Her mother gets up from the chair begrudgingly, and says, 'I'll visit you tomorrow, Noor. Without your dad. Would that be okay with you?'

Noor doesn't respond, doesn't look at her mother. Her sobs grow softer.

The mother sighs and saunters out of the room.

Simone says to the constable, 'Please wait outside. We need to talk to Noor.'

The constable nods and leaves, closing the door behind him.

Noor wipes away tears with the back of her hands. She reclines in bed and closes her eyes.

Simone motions Lucas to take a seat. She remains standing, watching Noor, waiting.

One minute. Two minutes. Simone continues to stare unblinkingly at Noor but doesn't say a word.

'It's creepy, you know . . . you staring at me like that,' says Noor, her eyes seemingly shut.

No reply.

Noor opens her eyes. 'Is this how you make people talk? I can tell you now that you are wasting your time, officer. It's not working.'

Simone doesn't say a word.

'Cool haircut, by the way,' says Noor. 'Maybe I should get myself that look. Shave it all off. Completely bald.'

'Why did you try to kill yourself, Noor?' asks Simone.

Silence.

Simone takes a step towards the bed, holding on to Noor's stare. 'What were you running away from, Noor? The cancer? The depression? Your parents? All the above?'

Noor's face turns ashen, jaw tightens and stare hardens. 'You don't know what you are talking about.'

Simone says, 'I tried to kill myself because of depression because I lost the only family I ever had. So, yes, I know what you are talking about. But, no, I don't know why you did it.'

Noor sits up in bed. Her expression softens—the crease on her forehead melts away, her mouth opens a tad bit, releasing the tension in her jaw. 'How did you do it?'

'Sleeping pills,' Simone responds without skipping a beat.

Noor nods. The edges of her mouth curl up into a smile. 'Tell me, are you happy to be alive?'

Simone shrugs her shoulders, doesn't reply. She is alive, but far from happy. *Happy* seems like a distant feeling, like a long-lost relative whom you used to know, but don't miss anymore. She doesn't miss being happy. She misses her just-lost relative: her grandma.

Noor says, 'It was all of the above.'

'What?'

'You asked me if it was cancer, depression, or parents? I was running away from all the above. And more. It felt like I was hanging from a cliff, clutching a tightrope, staring into the spiked rocks below, hoping someone would save me. And then I realized: I can save myself. I just need to cut the rope and end the agony. That's what I did.'

Simone nods without meaning to. She understands. She empathizes. It's funny how all her life people convinced her that she has a heart of stone, but here, now, she is empathizing with depression. It takes one to know one.

Simone clears her throat. 'You received a box. The *Dream Box*.' Simone forms air quotes with her fingers. 'It seems someone helped you cut the rope?'

Noor closes her eyes, inhales deeply. 'Yes. He did.'

'He? Who?'

'The Dreamcatcher.'

Simone and Lucas exchange a puzzled look.

'Who's the Dreamcatcher?' asks Lucas.

'I don't know. He reached out to me on Telegram. He—'

'What's Telegram?' Simone interjects.

Noor scoffs, shakes her head. 'Seriously, bro! Have you been living under a rock?'

'It's a messaging service like WhatsApp, but more secure.' Lucas comes to Simone's rescue.

Simone continues, ignoring the interlude. 'When did he first message you?'

'Umm . . . a month ago. He was suffering from cancer as well. Said he saw me in one of the support group sessions of the Dream Cancer Foundation.'

'Dream Cancer Foundation?'

'It's a pan-India support group of cancer patients.'

'Was your friend Sonali also a part of the support group?'

Noor nods, her face suddenly grim, sad at the mention of Sonali.

'So, the Dreamcatcher messaged you. Then what?'

Noor takes a deep breath. 'We could relate to each other. We struck a friendship. He was such a good listener.

He could totally understand what I was going through. And vice versa. Like soulmates.'

'Did he ever share his real name?'

'He never did. I never asked. Dreamcatcher—that's it.'

'Why did he send the *Dream Box*?'

'Isn't it obvious?'

Simone nods. 'I understand the purpose of the gauge-7 syringe. But there were other items that you were wearing when we found you. Rectangular earphones and a stick-on device called Dreamo. And then we found musk-scented candles in the room. I assume these items came from the box?'

'Yes.'

'But for what purpose?'

'To make it easier. To make the death less painful.'

'How did listening to songs or the smell of musk make it less painful?'

Noor sighs. 'Okay, let me explain. It's complex, so try to keep up.' She props herself up in bed and steeples her fingers, like a professor who is about to deliver a lecture. 'I wasn't listening to songs. I was on a call with the Dreamcatcher, listening to his voice while he hypnotized me in my sleep.'

Simone is stunned. *How can you hypnotize someone while they are sleeping? Remotely!* It is tough enough to hypnotize in person. It's a skill that takes years to learn, ages to master.

'But, how?' asks Simone.

'Have you heard of lucid dreams?'

'What dreams?' asks Simone.

'Lucid. Lucid dreams. You can Google it. It's when a person becomes aware that they are dreaming. You know the events flashing through your brain aren't really happening—it's a dream—but the dream feels vivid and real. It's like watching a movie that your brain has cooked up. You practice it often and you can control the unfolding of events in the dream. Then, you are no longer just watching the movie, you are also *directing* the movie.'

Noor pauses.

Simone is speechless, puzzled. A number of questions are swirling in her head, but none come to her lips.

Noor continues, 'And if you have lucid dreams with a master hypnotist, they can direct the movie in your brain—your dream—for you. That's why he calls himself the Dreamcatcher. He is the master of hypnosis through lucid dreaming.'

Lucas says, 'He hypnotized you to commit suicide while lucid dreaming?'

'Yes. Lucid dreaming is when your brain is most open to suggestions. It does whatever you—or in this case, the hypnotist—command it to do. It's the only time when your survival instincts switch off. You tell your brain to jump off a cliff in a dream and it'll obey you because it thinks you are only dreaming. It's not reality. So, in a way, you trick the brain.'

Simone mulls it over. 'So, did you try to commit suicide or did the Dreamcatcher try to kill you?'

'Both.' Noor smiles. 'Most depressed people want to kill themselves. But only some have the courage to take that final, fatal step. The Dreamcatcher holds your hand and helps you cross the river. You are the actor, but he directs the movie, tells you what to do. And you do it. Like I rammed the syringe full of air into my bloodstream. He asked me to do it while lucid dreaming. And I did it.'

Lucas asks, 'Why the candle?'

'It's a hallucinogenic drug. Makes it easier to lucid dream.' Noor shrugs her shoulders.

'And the stick-on device?'

Noor's eyes light up. 'Oh, the Dreamcatcher quite impressed me when he told me what it is. It's a device, like Fitbit. Tracks your brain activity while you are asleep and sends the data to him in real time. That's how he knows you've entered the dream state. That's how he knows the exact vulnerable moment when your brain would not resist the command of holding up the syringe and stabbing it in your neck.'

The gurgle and buzz of the air-conditioner take over as they all fall silent.

Simone is torn. Was this a suicide? Was this murder? As per law, it was an attempt to murder. Even though Noor permitted it, it was the Dreamcatcher who committed the deed. The sinful act was his and his alone. He manipulated and blindsided Noor. She needs help.

Simone says, 'Thank you for your time, Noor. We'll be in touch.'

Simone nods to Lucas, who gets up from the chair and follows Simone to the door.

'Officer,' says Noor.

Simone turns her head, her hand on the doorknob.

'I know what you think, but the Dreamcatcher is not a murderer. He was only trying to help to—'

'. . . to kill you.'

'Yes,' Noor swallows hard. 'But that's not murder. That's euthanasia.'

15

Simone and Lucas step out of the brightly lit hospital into the inky parking lot. Simone is quiet, lost in her thoughts, trying to solve the shuffled, messy Rubik's Cube puzzle that Noor shared.

Remote hypnosis? Lucid dreams? She is confused, lost. *How is it even possible?* But there is one thing she trusts with her life: Google. She pulls out her phone and starts googling.

'Crazy, right?' utters Lucas.

Simone doesn't respond. She is reading a research paper on how therapists in Germany employed lucid dreams to lower stress levels in clinically depressed patients.

'Why would someone go to such lengths to kill themselves?' Lucas muses.

'Pain,' Simone says without looking up from her phone. 'Most people don't fear death. They fear pain. Offer a painless death and you'd have a queue from here till India Gate with eager people jostling for a chance to go first.'

'Even cancer patients whose lives are nothing but pain and suffering?'

'Especially them. At least, some of them.' Simone looks up from her phone. 'They want to die, *and* they want to be pain-free one last time. It's like achieving Nirvana with your last breath. Then you can die in peace.'

They both grow quiet for a minute before Simone says, 'But here's my issue with the Dreamcatcher. He promises painless death, but it isn't painless, is it? He hypnotized them. It happened in their dreams, sure, but it's not painless.'

'What do you mean?' Lucas squints.

'An air embolism is quite painful. You've added an air bubble in your bloodstream, which leads to a stroke. The person would suffer sharp, stabbing pain in the chest, tremors and difficulty in breathing. It's not painless. The Dreamcatcher is promising painless deaths for these gullible girls. But he is only keeping half the promise. Death, only death—that's what he is offering them.'

'Yep, from the looks of it, he *is* murdering them.'

Simone shrugs her shoulders. 'He killed them. But I'm not sure if it's murder.'

'How so?'

'Euthanasia. It has been gnawing at me since Noor said the word. But if it's true, then aren't these suicides? Isn't it a charitable act? The victims wanted to die. They couldn't do it themselves, so they engaged the services of the Dreamcatcher.'

'So, he is selling death, which makes him a murderer, no?'

Simone nods. 'As per law, yes. But as someone struggling with depression, I'm not so sure.'

Lucas's face melts into a sad, concerned expression. Simone realizes that she just acknowledged her mental health struggles to Lucas, a colleague and a junior. She hasn't admitted it to anyone so far. People can see it, people can guess it, but she hasn't talked about it openly. Not even with her therapist. Suddenly, she feels naked, ashamed, as if a terrible secret is now on full public display.

Lucas touches Simone on the arm. 'We can talk about it if you want.'

Simone takes a step back, pulls away from his hand. 'The court has appointed a therapist for that.'

Slowly, Lucas drops his outstretched arm.

Simone shakes her head. 'I'm sorry. Thank you for the concern, Lucas. But can we get back to the case please?'

'Sure.' His tone is cold and professional. He clears his throat. 'The key question is—how do we catch the Dreamcatcher?'

Simone ponders over it and says, 'We start with the Dream Cancer Foundation, the cancer support group. That's his connection with the victims it seems. Both Noor and Sonali were part of this group. How about the other victims? Let's check with the Foundation. We need to get a list of the group members and start interviewing them.'

Lucas nods.

'And then, the matter of these Telegram chats. We know now that they were using Telegram to communicate. The Dreamcatcher remotely wiped off data from the victims' phones, but let's see if someone from IT can hack into their Telegram accounts. Plus, this time it's different.

We have a survivor. We ask Noor for her password—or get a warrant if she throws a hissy fit on privacy grounds—and access her Telegram account. See if it throws up any insights.'

'I'll get on it first thing tomorrow morning,' says Lucas.

'No, let's divide and conquer. You dig into the Dream Cancer Foundation. I'll get access to Noor's Telegram account and ask IT to hack into the others. Keep me posted if anything odd pops up.'

They bid goodbye. Lucas takes the Metro home. Simone offers to drop him at the Metro station, but Lucas declines. 'A little walk never hurt anyone,' he grins, winks at Simone, and walks away.

Alone in the parking lot, Simone's thoughts veer back to the brief episode, the panic attack she had earlier after entering the hospital. She even blurted out and admitted her depression to Lucas.

What's happening to me? I need help.

She takes out her phone and dials up the court-appointed psychologist, Dr Dia Sengupta.

'Hello,' Dia answers.

'Hello, Dr Sengupta.'

There is a pause as if Dia is trying to place the voice.

'It's good to hear from you again, Simone. Please call me Dia. How can I help you?'

'I need help, Dia. I need to see you. Now.'

'Now? I was about to go to bed and—' Dia pauses. 'Sorry, forget what I said. I know the last couple of months have been tough on you. And I'm here to help. Please come over.'

Simone checks her watch. It's ten minutes to eleven. She bites into her lower lip. 'Sorry, I didn't realize the time. How about tomorrow?'

'Don't worry about it, Simone. Come over now. I'll make us tea and we can chat.'

Simone shakes her head. She doesn't want to be an inconvenience at such a late hour. 'Tomorrow what time?' she presses.

Dia sighs. '8 a.m. tomorrow? I'll squeeze you in before my first appointment.'

'I'll be there.'

16

 **Audio Journal of *THE DREAMCATCHER*
Audio File #5**

How do you save someone who doesn't want to live?

You don't. If you truly care, you help them find a gun so they can shoot themselves in the mouth.

Sonali's cancer was growing like uncontrollable weeds in an untamed garden, curling around every nook, cranny and organ in the body. The doctors gave up. The painkillers gave up. She gave up. But I was determined to make her live. One more year. One more month. One more day. I was selfish. I wanted her for myself, all to myself. I was not ready to let her go.

I knew I couldn't fight cancer—it was a foregone conclusion. But I could fight her depression and her pain. For her. For me. I could dive into the deep, dark caverns of her mind and show her the fickle light of willpower. The will to fight, the will to live.

So, I researched and researched. Read scientific journals on willpower, studied neuroscience texts on tricking the mind, crammed psychological theses on happiness and learned hypnosis. And then, I found the solution: lucid dreams. So easy to learn, so difficult to master. But I was determined.

Now, you might wonder, as I did when I started, how does lucid dreaming help with depression? You become aware that you are dreaming while dreaming. But how does that awareness lower depression?

It's about one thing, and one thing alone: control.

People suffering from depression, post-traumatic stress disorder (PTSD) or anxiety, or acute stress disorder believe they have lost control. They are helpless, like a car on a highway whose brakes have failed, rattling at full speed, fated for a head-on collision. How would you feel inside that car? First, there'd be an adrenaline rush, fight or flight, your body's natural response. Soon, that adrenaline will turn into fear when you realize there is no way to stop the out-of-control car. And then comes a wave of resignation, acceptance of your fate because you realize the collision is inevitable. You have lost complete control. And hope. Then you either wait for the car to run its course, praying, helplessly strapped in your seat, until it collides with another—that's depression—or you drive it off a cliff yourself, ending the nightmare—that's suicide. It starts with helplessness; ends with your death.

Unless you regain control.

People suffering from depression—helpless in that out-of-control car—need to be reminded that they *still* have control. They can lower the gears, one at a time, to slow down the car or use a handbrake, or swerve the car into a soft, cushioned roadside barrier.

Lucid dreams help clinically depressed patients regain control. You, the dreamer, take control of the dream. You become the movie director. Go there, do this, fly, you tell yourself in the dream, and it happens. It gives you a sense of power, a sense of control. And then, when you open your eyes and come back to reality, you carry back that feeling of power because you remember; you were awake the whole time, aware of the dream.

I still remember the first time when Sonali woke up after a lucid dream. Her lazy, mocking smile told me it had worked. For a few moments, she was happy, upbeat, like she had conquered the world. She was chirpy the whole day, thriving on an undercurrent of positivity. But like any drug, the effect wore off the next day and she was back where she'd started.

And I realized. It is a drug, an addiction. And if I were to save Sonali, I had to get her addicted to lucid dreams.

17

Simone taps her police-issued boots on the polished hardwood floor, creating a squeaky sound that she finds irritating. But she can't stop stomping. She is nervous, uncomfortable and resigned, nervous to face Dia after the way she had bolted abruptly the last time she was here. She feels uncomfortable on the cushy three-seater sofa—she can't figure out why. There is a sense of resignation in her about making an appointment with Dia after the panic attack at the hospital yesterday. She is here now. Nowhere to run. *Or, maybe, I can run away like last time. Who is going to stop me?*

Simone gets up from the sofa, following her instincts.

'You aren't thinking of scurrying away like last time, are you?' Dr Dia Sengupta waltzes into the room, beaming, the pallu of her green-gold silk saree gently fluttering in her wake.

'Umm . . . no,' Simone says sheepishly and sits back down, hunched forward.

Dia settles into the wooden armchair. She has tied her hair into the same neat bun as last time. The glasses are different today—forest green, matching her saree.

'It's good to see you again, Simone.'

'I'm sorry about last time. And thank you for seeing me at such short notice.'

Dia flicks her hand. 'Don't mention it. Shall we pick up where we left off?'

Dia picks up her notebook.

Simone doesn't answer.

'Simone.'

'Yes?'

'You can stop tapping your feet now.' Dia smiles.

'Oh! Sorry.' Simone pushes her palms against her thighs and stops moving her feet.

Dia opens her notebook, reads her notes, and says, 'The last time you were here, you mentioned that you feel "dead inside" because your grandma, the only family you ever had, died.'

Simone stiffens, like a zookeeper does before entering the lion's cage. It dawns on her why she had run away the last time. She wants to get better. She wants to get rid of the panic attacks plaguing her. But she doesn't want to talk about her grandma. She doesn't want to talk about it, about anything, with a stranger. *Was it a mistake coming here again?*

'Can we talk about something else?' says Simone.

'What would you like to talk about?'

Simone clasps her hands together. They are sweaty. 'I had a panic attack at the hospital yesterday.'

Dia waits for her to continue.

Simone says, 'Is there any medication to make it go away?'

Dia ignores the question and asks, 'What did you panic about?'

Simone shrugs her shoulders. She doesn't want to talk about it. She doesn't want to dissect it. All she wants is a pill that can make it go away. Fast and easy.

Simone fidgets in her seat. 'I don't remember,' she lies.

Silence. Dia continues to stare at her, waiting for the truth.

'Umm . . . it reminded me of the last time I visited a hospital.'

'What happened the last time you were at the hospital?'

Isn't it obvious? Why does she want me to say everything out loud?

Simone says, 'Grandma died.'

'How did she die?'

Simone shakes her head. She doesn't want to relive that memory, even if it's just inside her head. 'I don't want to talk about it.'

Dia sighs, defeated.

Simone looks away, her eyes roving across the carpeted floor.

'You know what?' Dia nudges forward in her seat, her voice is cheery with excitement. 'Let's do a simple exercise. What are your thoughts about hypnosis?'

'Hypnosis?' Simone stiffens. 'Like controlling my mind and making me do what you want?'

Dia chuckles. 'Those are myths and misconceptions. I can't control your mind with hypnosis. I can't make you surrender your will. Think of it as a guided meditation. I'll be the guide. I'll help you relax your mind, but you'll be in charge. We can stop anytime you want.'

But that's not what they show in TV dramas.

'I'm here to help you. You can trust me, Simone. I've done guided meditations with all my patients. I can guarantee you'll feel relaxed and refreshed. And probably, no more panic attacks.'

No more panic attacks? It sounds good. Maybe worth a shot.

'Okay. Let's do it,' Simone says.

'Just sit back, close your eyes, and follow what I say.'

Simone sighs and closes her eyes.

'Take a deep breath in. Hold . . . and breathe out.'

Simone follows the instructions.

Suddenly, Simone hears the *ding* of a handbell, like those brass bells used for *aarti* at the temple.

'Now, breathe in and out when you hear the bell.'

Ding!

Simone takes a deep breath.

Ding!

She breathes out.

For the next five-ten minutes, Simone follows the bell, her breathing at its beck and call. Her breathing slows down, the tension in her muscles ebbs. She is floating in the air, light, cloud-like. She isn't sure if she is dreaming in deep sleep or still awake.

'Now, when you hear the bell, remove your boots, and lie down on the sofa. Make yourself comfortable.'

Ding!

Simone unties the boot laces and glides across the couch. It's like she is on autopilot. Her body followed the instructions while her mind was still floating in the clouds, relaxed and buoyant.

Ding!

Simone breathes in and out, without Dia saying a word.

'When you hear the bell now, imagine lifting an anvil off your chest. Use your hands, use your mind. Lift it.'

Ding!

Simone focuses her mind, pushes up with her hands.

'How do you feel?' asks Dia.

Simone smiles. She can't remember the last time she smiled this broadly, her lips apart, cheeks stretched to the eyes. 'Better. Better,' is all she can mouth.

'Let go of your inhibitions. Nothing can hold you back when you hear the next bell.'

Ding!

It imbues Simone with a rush of confidence. She is all-powerful. She is a ball of energy. Ready to conquer.

'Say I'm on top of the world.'

Ding!

Simone obeys. 'I'm on top of the world.'

'I'm not afraid of the truth.'

Ding!

'I'm not afraid of the truth.'

Dia whispers. 'Who raised you, Simone?'

Ding!

Simone is pulled back to the memories of sitting in her grandma's lap, listening to her stories about gods and demons, about giant creatures and tiny humans. 'My grandma,' she answers.

'What about your parents?' asks Dia.

Simone struggles to answer. But then, she hears the bell, clears her throat and says, 'I was adopted when I was very young. But my adopted parents died in a car accident.'

She never knew her birth parents or her adoptive parents. She doesn't even remember their faces. She was fortunate to have had four parents; unfortunate to never know, hug or love them. It's the reality she grew up with, the reality that shaped her childhood and defined her adulthood. But it's also the reality that turned out to be an illusion, a fabrication, a lie two months ago. Her birth mother is alive—well and truly alive. But Dia doesn't need to know that.

'So, your grandma raised you. Dadi or nani?'

Ding!

'Dadi. My adopted father's mother.'

Dia says, 'So, you lost your parents. Twice.'

Simone nods. A rush of sadness sweeps over her, like a fog out of nowhere on a chilly night.

'How did your grandma die?'

Simone goes numb. Her breathing escalates, her back tickles with sweat.

'Take a deep breath, Simone. Don't think of your grandma for a minute.'

Her breathing surges further. Images of her grandma—dead, unmoving, pale—flutter in front of her eyes like a movie. Human psychology—you tell the brain *not* to think of an elephant and that's all it does.

'Control your breathing. Relax.'

Ding!

Slowly, her heart rate subsides. Her breathing steadies.

'How did your grandma die, Simone?'

Ding!

Simone takes a breath. 'She was murdered.'

'Who murdered your grandma?'

Ding!

Simone doesn't reply. She wants to move her lips, but she can't. It's like they are sewn shut.

Ding! Ding!

'I killed my grandma.'

18

Lucas yawns. He tries to suppress it, covers his mouth with his palm, but the yawn comes out loud and long, inviting a side glance and grin from Inspector Gautami Pandey, who shares the cubicle with him at the CBI office.

'Long night?' Gautami asks.

Lucas blinks his eyes fervently. 'I barely slept.'

'Is Simone working you too hard on the case? From what I have heard, she can be a stone-cold slave master.'

'Na, Simone isn't too bad. She's like a coconut—hard on the outside, soft on the inside. You'd like her if you get to know her.'

'I doubt that. Where is she, by the way?'

'She had an appointment with her therapist, Dr Dia Sengupta. She'll be in later—' Lucas covers his mouth and lets out another yawn.

'If it isn't Simone, then why couldn't you sleep last night?'

'It's my teenage brother. *Sahebzaade* came home at midnight, drunk, out of his senses, and spent the night in the bathroom. I still can't forget the sight of his head dunked inside the toilet bowl and his arms hugging the bowl like a drowning man clinging to a lifebuoy.'

Gautami sniggers.

'I had to stay up the entire night, watching him, making sure he doesn't choke on his own vomit.'

'In a way, *accha hai*, it'll teach him a lesson to not do it again.'

Lucas nods, massages his temple. He doesn't mention that it has happened before. Many times. He has stopped counting.

Gautami switches the topic. 'I heard about your case. Another girl tried to commit suicide but survived?'

Gautami is the office gossip. But so is Lucas. He doesn't mind slipping information if he gets something in return. That is the first rule of gossip: you give some, you get some.

'Yeah, you won't believe it.' Lucas pulls his chair closer to Gautami's, his voice turning into a whisper. The second rule of gossip: what's shared in whispers is always true. 'These cases, these girls killing themselves, they are both suicides and murders.'

Gautami's eyes balloon. She grips Lucas's arm. 'What? How is it even possible?'

Lucas narrates what he heard from Noor last night— about remote hypnosis, lucid dreams and euthanasia.

Gautami sits back, dumbfounded. 'Crazy,' she says. 'So, what are you going to do?'

'For now, I'm digging into this cancer support group called the Dream Cancer Foundation. It's an online support group of over 300 members. Became quite active during the COVID lockdown, as you can imagine. I spoke with the Foundation's President this morning. She has promised to send me the list—'

Lucas's phone buzzes. It's an unknown number. He excuses himself and answers the call.

'Hello.'

'Inspector Lucas from CBI?'

'Yes, speaking.'

'I'm the assistant to the president of the Dream Cancer Foundation. I believe you spoke with her this morning. As requested, I have emailed you the complete list of our members and staff. We are happy to assist you in the investigation. Please let me know if there is anything else we can do.'

Lucas thanks her and disconnects.

'All well?' Gautami asks.

'Yes, yes. All good. Got the list.'

Gautami asks, 'You want to go out for a drink later tonight?'

Gautami likes him. He knows that. The last time they went drinking, she'd told him as much, tried to kiss him and then passed out at the bar. He'd dropped her home and slept on her sofa to make sure she was safe. The next morning, Gautami claimed she didn't remember a thing. He knows it isn't true. He also doesn't want a repeat. So, he says, 'Yeah, maybe. I'll let you know in the evening?'

Gautami frowns. 'Sure,' she says, turns away and returns to her work.

He will need to come up with an excuse. But, for now, he has work to do.

Lucas checks his email, downloads and opens the Excel sheet with the list from the Dream Cancer Foundation. It has two tabs, one for the patients and another for the staff. One by one, he types in the names of the murder-suicide victims. Each of them comes up on the list. He isn't surprised. But now, he is convinced that this is the pool in which the Dreamcatcher has been fishing.

He opens the tab with the list of staff members. It has two sub-lists of permanent and part-time staff.

Lucas yawns like a cat and stretches luxuriantly. He needs coffee.

He is about to get up from his chair when a name on the staff list hooks him. He blinks and zooms in the screen. The name doesn't change.

At the top of the list of part-time staff is a familiar name: Dr Dia Sengupta.

19

There is complete silence in the room, except for the deep humming of the fan rotating above their heads. Dia is looking at it, thinking and deciding how to proceed from here. Simone sits with her head in between her knees, unresponsive.

'Simone?'

Simone doesn't move or answer. She cannot believe she revealed her innermost thoughts to Dia. She had jerked awake the moment she realized what she had told Dia. *What happened to me? Why did I let my guard down?* Unrelenting tears flow and fall on the hardwood floor—the small pools turn it a darker shade of chocolate brown.

'Simone, why did you say you killed your grandma?' asks Dia.

No response.

'I received the police report. I know you didn't kill her. She died of a stroke.'

No response.

'Simone, take a deep breath. You can tell me.'

'I gave her that stroke!' yells Simone, rocking her head back up.

Dia purses her lips.

Simone sniffles. 'Sorry, I didn't mean to raise my voice.'

'It's okay. Let it out.'

Simone wipes her nose with the back of her palm. 'It was me. I am responsible for the stroke.'

'How? From my position and the forensics position, your grandma died of natural causes.'

'That's the perfect murder, isn't it?'

Dia doesn't respond.

'We were fighting the night she died. I was screaming at her, accusing her, threatening to leave her.' Simone scoffs. 'She raised me and there I was, willing to give up on her in an instant. So, you see? If I hadn't instigated the fight, she wouldn't have had a stroke and she'd still be alive. I'm responsible for grandma's death.'

'That's a huge burden to carry, Simone. You may have started the fight but that doesn't mean you killed your grandma.'

Simone shrugs her shoulders. 'I can't help it. That's just the way I feel.'

Dia shifts in her seat. 'Okay, tell me, what triggered the fight?'

Simone bites her lips. 'I wasn't completely honest with you earlier. I told you that my adoptive parents died in a car accident when I was very young. But my birth mother is alive.'

Simone lets it sink in, more for her than for Dia. She still can't wrap her mind around it.

She continues, 'Two months ago, I received a letter, a hand-written letter from my birth mother. So, you can imagine my disbelief. I didn't even know she was alive. So, I confronted grandma. I had so many questions. I wanted to know why she'd lied to me. Why was a little girl separated from her birth mother? Why, for all these years, my grandma—an honest, religious woman—was willing to live a lie.'

'And what did your grandma say?'

Simone bites her lower lip. 'Can we pause here? I don't want to talk about it.'

Dia closes her notebook and sits back. 'We can. But I want you to push through a little. I want you to let it out in one go. Think of it this way—what happens if you have had too much to drink and your—'

'I don't drink.' Simone interjects.

'Imagine someone who does. What does the body do after they've had too much?'

'Vomit.'

'All of it or half of it?'

Simone contorts her face. Dia could have given a less gross example.

Dia smiles. 'Ew, right!' She leans forward. 'But that's how the body reacts. It's all in or all out. Same with mental stress. You've to let it all out for the mind to heal.'

Simone nods.

'So, what did your grandma say when you confronted her?' Dia asks.

'She tried to hide it first. Said it was untrue. But when I showed her the letter from my mother—especially the envelope, which had the sender's address—I could see it in her eyes. Grandma had been lying. She said she was trying to protect me from that "despicable woman"—my mother. And then she got angry. Said I should burn the letter or soak it or tear it into tiny shreds. When I disagreed, she tried to snatch it away from my hands,' says Simone, her eyes staring at the blank wall behind Dia, reliving the events of that day.

'What did your birth mother say in the letter?'

Simone peels her eyes away from the wall and glances at Dia. 'You can read it. I have it with me. For some reason, I have been carrying it since I received it. Maybe because it's the only proof I have of my mother's existence.' She unbuttons the breast pocket of her police uniform and takes out a crumpled envelope that has been folded many times over. She removes a single page from the envelope, gets up, and hands it to Dia.

It's a standard A4 white paper, creased and wrinkled. Dia pushes back her glasses and starts reading the letter written in fine cursive handwriting.

My dearest Simmi,

It has been twenty-four years since I last saw you. You were wearing an orange frock that I had sewn at home before you were born. I remember it was cotton with lace borders and had tiny little white lilies imprinted all over. Oh, how lovely you looked! Chubby and ruddy and cutesy! You were a happy baby, always smiling. Oh, I was in love, so much in love with you, my darling girl. You were my one ray of sunshine, one and only.

You were a year old then. So, you might not remember me, might not have even heard of me from your adopted family. But I am your mother, your birth mother.

I saw your photo in the newspaper the other day— tall, beautiful, confident. Shaved head suits you :-) The newspaper mentioned that you solved the case of The Girl in the Glass Case in Bhopal. I am so proud of you! You know, even before I read your name in the article, I knew it was you. I just knew. It gladdens my heart so much to see that you've become an accomplished IPS officer.

Simmi, I'm not sure what your adopted family has told you, but I had my reasons to stay away from you for this long; reasons that I sometimes regret. Only sometimes, because it was necessary and much needed. I had to give you away. It had to be done. To protect you. Trust me, I have had twenty-four years to think about it and I'm convinced that it was the right step. Your dadi or the police will not agree, but they are not the ones I want to convince. You are.

Come and see me, Simmi. It's a plea from a mother to her daughter. We have much to talk about.

Love, all of it,
Your Mumma
PS: Don't let the address on the envelope dissuade you.

Dia folds the letter. Hands it back to Simone.

'What did your mother do that was so necessary?'

Simone fidgets with the letter, weighing her thoughts. *Should I tell her? Well, I have come this far. No going back now.*

Simone hands over the envelope to Dia. 'Read the sender's address.'

Dia twirls the envelope in her hand. She gasps. 'Tihar Jail?'

Simone pulls in her breath, the truth squeezing at her stomach muscles. 'Yes, my birth mother is in jail. Serving life imprisonment.'

'But, why?'

'. . . because she killed her husband, my father.'

20

Simone steps out from the cool bungalow into Delhi's searing heat. It's only 10 a.m., but she is exhausted. The session with Dia has wrenched out every ounce of energy.

She walks the length of the massive courtyard and exits from the front gate. The constable on sentry duty pulls up his face mask hurriedly before Simone reprimands him again. Simone has no energy to scold or lecture. She gives him a soft nod, saunters to the Jeep and climbs inside. She pushes her head against the headrest and closes her eyes.

Her thoughts veer to her mother, her birth mother. Twenty-four years in jail—that's a lot of time. For some, it's a lifetime.

She deserves it, thinks Simone. What else was she expecting when she killed her husband? But why did she do it? Didn't she realize that Simone—less than a year old then—would become an orphan? What mother does that to her child?

Dia had encouraged her to keep an open mind and meet her mother in prison. She'd lashed out at Dia. *Why?*

Why should she meet the woman who abandoned her newborn child?

It's the letter. The culprit, the source of all her misery. If she hadn't received the letter, her grandma would still be alive. If she hadn't received the letter, she wouldn't have swallowed those damn sleeping pills and then later, be forced to discuss her private affairs with a therapist.

Simone rips open her chest pocket, pulls out the letter, crumples it into a ball and flings it out of the Jeep window with all her might. She is panting from the effort.

Simone sighs. She shouldn't be littering the street. She can't be a rule-breaker herself.

'Fuck!' she yells, attracting the attention of the constable at the gate, who averts his gaze immediately.

Simone steps out of her Jeep, picks up the ball of paper on the pavement, and pockets it. She'll burn it at home, she decides.

Her mobile phone rings. She fishes it out. It's Lucas.

'Tell me?' she blurts.

'Well, good morning to you too,' says Lucas. Simone imagines his dimply grin. She purses her lips before she says something she'll regret later.

When Simone doesn't reply, Lucas clears his throat and says, 'I found something interesting on the list from the Dream Cancer Foundation. Get this—your therapist, Dia Sengupta, is a part-timer there.'

'So?' says Simone.

'No, I just thought it was interesting, a coincidence.'

'She's a therapist. She helps terminally ill patients deal with depression. It's not interesting, it's expected,' says Simone.

Lucas is tight-lipped.

'Anything else?' she asks curtly.

'Umm . . . yes, I have also asked them for a sub-list of people who attended the group therapy sessions with the victims. My hunch is that the Dreamcatcher encountered the victims during these group sessions.'

'Good. Get the list and start interviewing. I suggest you start with people who attended the sessions with Sonali and Noor. They were best friends; they might have attended the same sessions. The Dreamcatcher must have found them during one of those sessions.'

'Will do,' says Lucas and hangs up.

Simone turns on the ignition and puts the Jeep in gear. It's time to visit Noor again and read her secret Telegram chats with the Dreamcatcher.

21

 Audio Journal of *THE DREAMCATCHER*
Audio File #6

I've always wondered about the moment, the exact moment when the dream begins. You know, when you lie in bed, put your head on the pillow and go from reality one moment to a dream state the next. Think about it! Does it start abruptly, or does it simply fade in? I can guarantee it's a blur for you. You can't pinpoint the exact moment of transition.

Sonali and I spoke at length about the moment when a dream begins. She believed it was a blur because it is a wavy, hazy transition—kind of like the twirling, fuzzy way old movies would transition to flashbacks. You are in the real world, then your head spins like a spindle and—poof!—you are now in dreamland.

Bullshit!

It isn't like a flashback. It isn't a fade-in. Trust me, I've ventured into more lucid dreams than the times I've gotten laid. It's a transition, yes, but it's a transition from a static image to an animation. It's about movement. Most dreams start as a static representation of your own room. Your eyes are closed but you can picture your room in your head—the clock ticking, the breeze from the fan flowing over your face, your phone charging on the bedside table—but it's covered in a mist-like haze, a sort of vignette on a frame. The dream starts when your subconscious powers up and converts that static image into an animation. Sort of like creating animations in Adobe Photoshop. The image is the starting point of the dream. The animation takes the dream forward and makes it into a movie.

Why am I telling you this? Because you need an anchor when dreaming lucidly. It's important to know when the dream begins. You need to become aware to take control over your subconscious, guide it, manoeuvre the dream and take it for a spin.

Confused?

Okay, let me give you a simple test you can perform to wake up in your dream. *Run into a wall.* Yep, that's it! Run into a wall—if you bang your head, can't pass through, it's reality. But if you pass through, as if you are a ghost, my friend, it's time to wake up in your dream, realize you are dreaming and do whatever the fuck you want. It's your dream, your movie.

22

Simone enters the hospital with trepidation, half expecting another panic attack. But the hospital doesn't seem as intimidating during the day as it did last night when the lights, the empty corridors, had overwhelmed her. Today, the yellowing wallpaper, the rusting waiting area chairs, and the worn-out crowd make it look defeated, commonplace. Yesterday, the caustic smell of antiseptic had assaulted her senses; today it smells clean, pure.

She climbs the stairs and walks to Noor's room. A turbaned Sikh man with a moustache that extends from one ear to the other has replaced the constable from last night, watching over Noor, making sure she doesn't attempt suicide again. The constable salutes Simone. She salutes back and asks, 'Is the victim awake?'

He nods.

Simone knocks on the door.

'Come in,' says a feeble voice.

Noor is sitting up in bed, fiddling with her phone.

'How are you?'

Noor shrugs her shoulders, her eyes glued to the phone screen, her fingers tapping away.

Simone walks to her bedside and realizes that Noor is engrossed in a mobile game. 'What are you playing?'

Noor doesn't respond.

Simone tilts her head closer. It's a shooting game where players are trying to kill each other. Suddenly, a bullet hits Noor's avatar right in the head and blood splatters on the phone screen. Game over.

'No, no, no! Fuck!' Noor cries and slams the phone on the mattress. 'You distracted me. I was so close!' she stares at Simone, her bloodshot eyes prickled with annoyance.

Simone sits down on the chair meant for visitors. 'What were you playing?'

'PUBG.'

Simone nods blankly. She knows it's a widely popular video game, but games and Simone have never gotten along. She couldn't care less. 'Did you get any sleep last night?'

Noor massages her eyes with the heels of her palms. 'No, I couldn't sleep.'

'Couldn't or wouldn't?'

'How does it matter, officer? Why are you here? I told you everything you needed to know.'

'Not everything.'

Simone picks up the phone that Noor had slammed. It's new, the metallic edges gleaming despite the dull light. 'New phone?'

'Of course. You guys confiscated my iPhone as evidence when you found me. Mom bought me a new one when she visited me in the morning today.'

'Where is your mom?'

'Gone.'

'Gone? Where?'

Noor sits back and sighs loudly. 'Returned to Mumbai. She has a meeting with a Bollywood socialite client in the evening. She has to be there. How will we pay the house bills otherwise?'

'And your dad?'

Noor becomes visibly irritated. 'Why are you here, officer?'

Simone feels for Noor—young, alone, and depressed. She tried to commit suicide yesterday, and her family has all but abandoned her today. There is nothing more heartbreaking than the indifference of loved ones when you need them most. The opposite of love is not hate; it's indifference. Simone doesn't remember her own parents. But she'd rather not have parents than suffer through their apathy like Noor.

Simone hands the phone to Noor. 'I want to read your chats with the Dreamcatcher.'

Noor swallows hard. Her bony collarbones heave up and down, once. 'It's private and embarrassing,' murmurs Noor, not meeting Simone's gaze.

'It's a police matter now, Noor. Best that you cooperate.'

Noor ponders over it, still not meeting Simone's eyes. '. . . sure, why not,' she says with resignation.

Noor taps a few times on her phone and signs into Telegram. 'Please don't read the other chats. They're private.'

Simone isn't interested in teenage gossip or teenage crushes or teenage whining. She's only interested in the Dreamcatcher. But she understands. She understands how it feels to share intimate, private details with a stranger. It's how she feels with her therapist.

Suddenly, Noor's jaw tightens, her eyes narrow. She scrolls up and down on her phone screen. 'That's odd,' she says.

'What?'

'I can't find any of my chats. The chat with him should be right at the top. He was the last person I communicated with before I . . .' Noor purses her lips. She can't bring herself to complete the sentence. 'But all my chats have disappeared.'

Simone knows they haven't disappeared. They have been deleted. It wouldn't be hard to do for someone capable of wiping phones clean remotely after killing his victims.

'See if you can send him a new message,' says Simone.

Noor brightens up at the idea as if she'd lost a friend and Simone had suggested a way to find him. She taps a few times on the screen. Her expression turns grave again. 'I can't find him. I can't find anybody. My contact list is empty.'

The gurgle and buzz of the air-conditioner take over as they both fall silent.

Simone frowns. She was hoping to gain insight into the Dreamcatcher's psyche, or maybe a clue that reveals his identity. But this lead has turned cold.

Simone sighs. She's done here. But before she goes, she wants to help Noor. She rummages in her pocket, takes out a visiting card and hands it to Noor. 'Call her. She's a clinical psychologist. She'll be able to help you.'

'Like a therapist? I don't need a therapist.'

'You don't have a choice, Noor. The court will mandate you to undergo therapy. I know because I was in your position. Actually, I am in your position.' Simone scoffs. 'That's why I'm recommending the therapist. Not as a police officer, but as someone who understands what you are going through.' She points to the card. 'Call her. She's one of the best in Delhi. Unless you want your parents to select the therapist for you?'

At the mention of her parents, Noor grabs the card as if it's a lifeline. 'Thank you,' she says and reads the card. 'Dr Dia Sengupta?' Her brow furrows.

Simone remembers what Lucas told her. 'Do you know Dr Sengupta?' she asks.

'Yes, of course. Dr Sengupta moderated a couple of our group therapy sessions at the Dream Cancer Foundation. She's top-notch. Her sessions on lucid dreaming helped so many of us deal with depression.'

Simone is stumped. *Lucid dreams?* She didn't know Dia taught lucid dreaming. Her heart paces like a piston.

'Lucid dreaming? As in the lucid dreaming that the Dreamcatcher used to murder his victims?' Simone narrows her eyes.

Noor bites her lips. 'I shouldn't have mentioned it. It's not what you think, officer. Yes, Dr Sengupta taught us lucid dreaming. But it was to help us manage depression. She can't be the Dreamcatcher.'

'Why can't Dia be the Dreamcatcher?'

Noor opens her mouth, but no words come out. She has no answer.

23

'State your name, please,' says Lucas.

'Srishty Pandey,' says the girl on the other end of the call. Her voice is soft, musical, almost like a cuckoo bird, as if on the verge of breaking into a song.

Lucas fiddles with his earphones. This is his fifth interview for the day with members of the Dream Cancer Foundation. Simone had called him earlier and asked him to prioritize the interviews with members who had attended Dia's sessions. Lucas was taken aback. Simone hadn't blinked an eye when he'd found out the connection between Dia and the foundation. She had defended Dia. But now, Simone had a change of heart. She wanted to dig deeper into Dia.

And, boy, was she right! Every interview since had confirmed Dia's connection with lucid dreams. And more.

Lucas says into the phone. 'Srishty, let me remind you that this call is being recorded in case I need to revisit what you share with me today.'

'Sure.'

'How did you come across the Dream Cancer Foundation?'

'Umm . . .' Srishty thinks for a while before answering. '. . . last year, I was diagnosed with breast cancer, and I went into a deep depression. Who has breast cancer at eighteen, right?'

Lucas stays mum.

Srishty continues. 'I was supposed to start college—BSc in chemistry at Christ University, Bengaluru—but I didn't. My parents persuaded me to take a gap year. I was a mess. I used to cry for no reason at all, wail as if a family member had died. I just couldn't understand why God had punished me for no reason. Why me?'

Srishty pauses.

'It was my aunt who suggested I join a support group of cancer patients. Initially, I had laughed at the idea. For me, support groups were Alcoholics Anonymous and Narcotics Anonymous . . . meant for addicts. At least, that's the image I had in my mind. I didn't want to meet strangers and share my life story. I have friends for that, no?'

Lucas remains quiet.

'But then, mom suggested I try an online support group. I wouldn't have to leave the house and if I didn't like it, I could stop anytime. Mom did the research and found out about the Dream Cancer Foundation. I attended a session, liked it. Then COVID hit. It became even more easy to attend their online sessions. So, I kept the habit.'

'What did you do in those sessions?'

'Depends,' says Srishty. 'Some involved sharing and listening to each other's stories. Some were teaching sessions. The foundation would bring in experts— psychologists, spiritual gurus, hypnotists—to help us deal with our problems. Some were inspirational sessions where they'd bring in people who had beaten all odds to defeat cancer. You know, to lift our spirits, to encourage us.'

Lucas nods. It was time to weave in the two key questions.

'Did anyone named the Dreamcatcher attend those sessions?'

'Dreamcatcher? That's somebody's real name?'

'Well, it could be. It's a free country,' says Lucas matter-of-factly.

'It's catchy, but no, don't remember anyone named the Dreamcatcher in any of the sessions.'

Lucas bobs his head and moves to the next key question. 'Do you remember a session with Dr Dia Sengupta?'

'Oh, yes!' Srishty brightens up, her voice rising in tempo. 'That was one of the best sessions I attended. She taught us new techniques to deal with depression, gave us practical advice and even mentored some of us one-on-one after the session. She is truly an inspiration. Brilliant, simply brilliant.'

'What did she teach?'

'Umm . . . guided meditation, self-hypnosis and lucid dreaming.'

Lucas is intrigued. He wants to ask about lucid dreaming as planned, but *self-hypnosis*?

'What's self-hypnosis?'

'Exactly what the name suggests. You give yourself positive reinforcement to accomplish a goal and become highly focused and completely absorbed in the present. It's like the movie, *3 Idiots*. You say—'all is well, all is well'—to yourself over and over again. And soon, you believe it.'

'You mentioned some of you took a one-on-one session with Dr Sengupta afterwards. Did you?'

'Yes,' she says, her voice enunciating the 's' almost musically—a yesss! 'Actually, I connected with her twice afterwards.'

'For what?'

'I started to practice lucid dreaming. But it was difficult to achieve on most nights. I was going nowhere. So, Dr Sengupta helped me out.'

'How?'

'She asked me to keep a dream journal, taught me how to induce lucid dreams, showed me how to wake up in the dream and take control of it. She even hypnotized me the first time to help me out.'

'What?' Lucas sits up in his chair.

'Yeah, she hypnotized me, over the video call. She's quite good at it.'

Lucas is stumped, his mouth agape.

Srishty continues, 'But I was no good at lucid dreaming. So, before our second session, she couriered a stick-on device to me. She said it'd help induce lucid dreams, and I'd be able to track my dreams like you track your daily steps on FitBit.'

Lucas shoots up on his feet, his mouth dry, his heart racing. 'Do you remember the brand name of the device?'

'Umm . . . she mentioned it was from a German research company.'

She pauses. Lucas's heartbeat pauses with her, even though he knows what's coming.

'Ah, yes! It's called Dreamo.'

24

Dia pins the pleats of her azure-blue pure georgette saree in place. Not one pleat is out of place; each pleat is of the same size and equidistant from the next. For today, she has chosen aqua blue earrings, pale blue eye shadow, and spectacles that match the blue shimmer in her saree, like sun rays sparkling off a calm blue ocean. Dia steps back and looks at her reflection in the full-length mirror. Elegant, professional, organized—that's how she wants to be seen and remembered by her patients, and that's how she looks, always. Today, though, is special. It's not for her patients, it's for the police.

Dia twists and turns and twirls in front of the mirror, and nods in satisfaction, admiring how the saree brings out her otherwise angular curves. Despite no wrinkles on the saree, she brushes her fingers against her thighs, smoothing and caressing the soft fabric. It's wrinkle-free georgette, but Dia had ironed the saree before wearing it—a habit she picked up from her mother.

Ah, sweet mother. May she rest in peace.

Dia misses her mum sometimes. She misses their evening chai sessions. Mum venting and ranting in her raspy, manly voice. She misses the way mum used to say 'tch, tch' when talking about almost anyone. As a life principle, her mother hated more than she loved. Especially during her last days. People attributed her wretchedness to the cancer in her throat. But Dia knew it was mum being mum—sceptical, selfish and spiteful. It's funny, thinks Dia, because mum spent her entire adulthood working as a student counsellor in a local school. She used to help aimless, gullible and innocent kids. It's the only job she ever had, and yet, somehow, to cross that sea of innocence, mum had built a boat of bitterness.

A flash of anger passes through Dia's eyes. She sees her eyes turn narrow, tetchy in the mirror, seething with resentment.

Bitter, bitter, bitter—that's how she remembers the three years of her life spent caregiving to that wretched human. She doesn't miss mum anymore. She misses the wasted three years—snatched, taken, gone!

Dia was preparing for medical exams when mum was first diagnosed with cancer. Stage four, laryngeal cancer, 30 per cent survival rate. It had spread from her throat to the liver, from the lymph nodes to her bones. When the doctor asked mum why she hadn't come earlier for a check-up, mum scoffed and told him she thought it was a mild sore throat—a sore throat that lasted one full year. While it ached non-stop and her voice became permanently hoarse, mum kept popping Strepsils instead of visiting a doctor. Mum was determined that way, determined to follow her own advice, no matter how misguided or childish. After she was diagnosed, mum embraced the bed with the same tenacity she'd popped Strepsils. She didn't need to—the doctor had even advised her against it to prevent bedsores and muscle atrophy—but mum remained bedridden at home. It was like she channelled all her willpower to never leave the bed. Ever. Not even for her weekly chemo sessions. She had to be carted to and from the hospital on a stretcher. Not even for nature's calls; someone had to clean up after her.

Dia grimaces and gags, remembering the putrid, sickly smell that was ever present in mum's room.

No nurse lasted for more than a week. Mum made sure of it. Dia secretly thought mum was doing it get her husband's attention, which had been waning for a while. But after six weeks and nine nurses, Dia's father—who couldn't be bothered to take time from his rising political career for such 'trivial matters'—decided it was best for Dia to take a break from school and nurse her mother at home. *Why does a girl need education, anyway?* is how he saw it. Dia fought him. He resisted and persisted. They agreed for six months. It lasted three years.

It would have lasted longer, much longer, if I had not intervened.

Suddenly, a knock on the door pulls Dia from her reverie. 'Come in,' she says.

Radhika, her assistant, pushes the door ajar, squeezes her head through, and says, 'Ma'am, the CBI officers are here.'

'Make them sit in the office. I'll be right there.'

Radhika nods, pulls out her head and closes the door behind her.

Dia swivels and looks at herself in the mirror one last time. She is ready. Ready to face the police officers and their pointed questions. She needn't worry. She has done nothing wrong.

* * *

'Do you think we have enough evidence to arrest Dia?' Lucas asks Simone, sitting next to her on the sofa in Dia's office.

'No.' Simone runs a hand over her head, the tiny bristles prickling against her palm. Her head needs a fresh shave. 'All we know is that she teaches lucid dreaming, is a trained hypnotist and gave Dreamo devices for free to members at the Dream Cancer Foundation. And besides, the witness account from Noor identifies the Dreamcatcher as a man.'

'Shall we at least bring her in for questioning?' pleads Lucas.

Simone ponders over the question. 'No, we need concrete evidence. Plus, I don't want to spook her if she is indeed the Dreamcatcher. Remember, she's the daughter of a cabinet minister. It'll be politicized too fast, too soon. We'll be off the case even before we can lay a finger on Dia.'

Lucas scoffs. 'Not just we. The CBI will be off the case if a cabinet minister gets involved.'

Simone nods, fully understanding what Lucas means. The CBI is a Central Government agency. A cabinet minister in the Central Government has enough clout to disrupt the agency's function.

At that moment, Dia waltzes into her office. Simone and Lucas stand up to greet her.

'Hello, officers. Please take a seat,' she says with a broad smile and flops down on the armchair with a flourish, crosses one leg over the other and sits back. The soft, gleaming *pallu* of her saree settles down after her with a whispered whoosh.

Simone settles down on the sofa. Lucas settles down next to her, slowly, as if in slow motion. He can't take his eyes off Dia. He doesn't want to. He is enchanted, infatuated. Dia has the elegance of a charming celebrity and the assuredness of a start-up founder. She is impeccably dressed. Her hair has a natural lustre. Her skin glows from within as if emanating a light of her own. Lucas can't make out if Dia is wearing make-up. But who cares?

It's the first time Lucas is meeting Dia in person. He hopes it isn't the last.

Suddenly, Dia is looking right at him. Her eyes steady on him, her moist lips spread into a grin that revs up a flutter deep in his belly. She says something to him. But his foggy, occupied brain doesn't register the words flowing out of her luscious, pink lips.

Simone nudges him with her elbow.

'Umm . . . sorry, what?' he says, snapping out of the trance.

Dia chuckles. 'I was asking your name, officer.'

'Lu . . .' He clears his dry throat. 'Lucas. My name is Lucas.' The words tumble out, toppling over one another. In the corner of his eye, Lucas sees Simone shaking her head.

'Nice to meet you . . . Lucas.' Dia mutters his name with a provocative little pout that makes her lips look like two plump red cherries. His heart melts.

Dia turns to Simone and says, 'You mentioned over the phone that you had questions for me about the suicides you are investigating. Tell me, how can I help?'

Simone hunches forward. 'Are you aware of the Dream Cancer Foundation, Dia?'

'Yes, I volunteer with them a few times a month.'

'That's noble. Very noble,' Lucas nods with enthusiasm and keeps nodding till a glare from Simone makes him control his bobbing head.

Dia peers at him and smiles. 'Thank you, Lucas. I do what I can to help the people who need me.'

I need you, thinks Lucas and nearly blurts it out. He shakes his head, trying to get a grip on his wild, untethered infatuation with Dia. He came here convinced that Dia is the Dreamcatcher. But now, for some reason, he wants to catch Dia in his dreams, and never let her go.

'Volunteer in what capacity?' Simone asks.

Dia shrugs. 'Sometimes, I moderate group therapy sessions. Sometimes, I teach the members. And sometimes, I do one-on-one therapy sessions.' Dia peers at Lucas, unblinking, directly into his eyes.

Lucas looks away, shy, abashed, like a teenager who's been caught staring at his high school crush.

'What do you teach the patients?' asks Simone.

'Many things.' Dia sits back, relaxed. 'Techniques, tools, therapies to help them strengthen their mental health.'

'Like lucid dreaming?'

A warm smile spreads across Dia's face, like a skipping stone creating a ripple in a lake. 'Yes, like lucid dreaming,' she says.

'And hypnosis?'

'Of course, it's my speciality.'

Simone shifts in her seat uneasily and clears her throat, remembering her last hypnosis session with Dia, but too embarrassed to discuss it in front of Lucas. She brings Dia back to her line of questioning. 'Did you distribute a few devices, coin-sized stick-on patches, named Dreamo to people at the foundation?'

'Yes. Not a few though. I have given out many. Free of cost, of course.'

'What for?'

'Dreamo is a breakthrough, a state-of-the-art technology. It both triggers and tracks lucid dreams in real-time.' Dia leans forward. 'Look, it takes practice and months to induce lucid dreams at will. Most patients who are struggling with clinical depression are novices. They find it hard to trigger lucid dreams. They need help. Immediate help. Dreamo gives faster results.'

'How many Dreamo devices have you distributed to date, give or take?'

Dia glances at the ceiling and narrows her eyes, thinking, calculating. 'Twenty. Maybe thirty.'

Simone pauses and glances at Lucas. Lucas knows the question that's coming next. The clincher, the surprise, the bombshell—the question that'll rouse Dia.

Simone asks, 'And, Dia, did you help six terminally ill girls commit suicide with Dreamo?'

'Excuse me!' Dia sits up. The smile vanishes from her face. 'Are you accusing me of murder, ASP Singh?'

Lucas notices the use of Simone's formal title. The flimsy veneer of informality and kinship has suddenly vanished—like when a cobweb disappears as if it has been splashed with water.

'Depends on the answer to that question, Ms Sengupta,' Simone retorts. 'Did you or did you, not aid or abet in the suicides?'

'No. Of course not.' Dia's voice is even and composed. 'I don't even understand how Dreamo can kill anybody. It's like Fitbit. It's harmless.'

'We cross-checked with the German manufacturer of Dreamo. Can you tell us why we found six Dreamos that you had purchased . . .' Simone points a finger at Dia. '. . . at all six crime scenes?'

'How would I know? I'm not responsible for the devices that I gave away. As I said, I handed out about thirty Dreamos. I have no idea how six of those landed at your crime scenes. None whatsoever.'

Silence.

There it was. The stumbling block, the barrier that Lucas and Simone couldn't get past—Dia's plausible deniability. They had discussed it before coming here. But

Simone wanted to stir up Dia, shake the tree and see if any apples fell.

'I'm sorry for the direct question, Dia. I had to ask,' says Simone.

Dia waits for a breath. 'I understand,' she says finally. She looks away, her voice drops. 'But it's quite disconcerting that, somehow, unknowingly, I've played a part in the suicides of the very girls I was trying to help. They were my patients, my students, my responsibility.'

Lucas feels for Dia. He wants to reach out, hold her hand, squeeze it, comfort her, and tell her she is not responsible. She was only trying to help. He believes her.

'Dia, can you give us a list of the people who received Dreamos from you?' asks Simone.

'Yes, certainly. Anything to help.'

Simone nods, glances at Lucas and jumps to her feet. 'Then I think we are done. Thank you for your time, Dia.'

* * *

'Do you believe her?' Simone asks Lucas once they step out of the bungalow into the searing summer heat.

Lucas rolls up his shirt sleeves. 'Yes, it doesn't look like she'd do such heinous crimes.'

Simone looks at him from the corner of her eye. 'When did we start absolving alleged criminals for their good looks?'

'No, all I'm saying is that . . . that . . .'

'What, Lucas?' Simone stops and crosses her arms.

'That . . . she is a gracious lady. Her intentions are noble. She engages in philanthropic work—helps kids suffering from cancer. And you saw how devastated she was that the devices she bought played a role in the suicides.'

'So, we drop her as a suspect because she is *gracious*, and because you have a crush on her?'

Lucas tuts his lips. 'What? Crush on her? Me? No! Not at all.'

Simone keeps glaring at him.

'Was it that obvious?' Lucas smiles, accentuated by his dimples, scratching his head absent-mindedly.

'Keep it professional, Lucas. Keep it professional.' Simone walks away towards the Jeep before Lucas says another word.

Lucas saunters after Simone and jumps in on the passenger side. They sit in silence for a few moments before Lucas says, 'What about you? Do you believe her?'

Simone thinks it over and sighs loudly. 'Yes. Can't say I trust her. But I don't doubt her.' She pauses. 'The good news is that we now have a shortlist of people who received Dreamos from Dia. I bet it's one of them.'

'Or some of them,' says Lucas.

'What do you mean?' asks Simone.

'I have a theory,' he says.

'Go on.'

'Maybe because I was busy finding reasons to vindicate Dia, it hit me that multiple people received those devices from Dia. Multiple people could have come together to help each other.'

'Help each other?' asks Simone.

'Remember what Noor said—it's euthanasia, not murder. We are dealing with terminally ill, clinically depressed teens who want to end their lives. All they need is the last painless push off the cliff. Think about it—who understands their pain, their suffering? The kids who are like them. Kids in the same boat. Kids burdened with cancer and depression. Kids who see euthanasia as an act of charity.'

Lucas pauses.

'What if some of those kids banded together, pooled the devices they had received from Dia, and created the Dreamcatcher character to euthanize their friends?'

25

In the last year, Dia moderated twelve sessions, one each month, at the Dream Cancer Foundation. One hundred and seventy-four members attended those sessions, a higher-than-average turnout owing to COVID lockdowns and the pan-India presence of the Foundation. Simone and Lucas have spent the entire week doing telephonic interviews with those members. They have interviewed ninety-six people so far. Plenty more to go.

The interviews have confirmed what they already know. The members, Dia's patients, adore her and consider her a true inspiration. She teaches lucid dreaming and self-hypnosis. She is a gifted therapist and an even better hypnotist. So far, twenty-one members have admitted to receiving the Dreamo device from Dia, which she sent by courier. They couldn't stop singing her praises during the interviews. Most credit Dia for helping them escape the deep, dark dungeon of depression. Few even credit Dia for overcoming suicidal intentions.

Simone questions if she was right to doubt her therapist. Maybe Dia isn't the Dreamcatcher after all. Or maybe Lucas's theory of a gang of murderers holds more merit than the earnestness she's shown for it.

Simone reads the next name on her interview list: Avni Basumatary, an eighteen-year-old Guwahati resident suffering from leukaemia, blood cancer.

Simone's shoulders sag. Interviewing cancer patients for a week has taken a toll on her. She also feels empty, miserable, as if there's a grey cloud hovering over her head, persistently showering her with stinging drops of despair.

Simone inhales deeply, picks up the phone and calls the number mentioned against Avni's name.

'Hello,' a tired, dry voice answers the call.

'Hi, is it Avni Basumatary?'

'Yes.' The word drools out of Avni's mouth at the other end of the line.

'This is ASP Simone Singh from the CBI. I'm calling regarding a criminal case we are investigating. Would you have five–ten minutes to answer some questions?'

'How did you get my number?'

Avni's directness takes Simone by surprise. 'We received phone numbers of all members of the Dream Cancer Foundation, courtesy of a court warrant. Your phone number included.'

'Which criminal case?'

'Sorry?'

'You mentioned earlier that it's regarding a criminal case. Which one?'

Avni seems to be the passionately curious kind, thinks Simone. Most people she's interviewed so far immediately agreed to answer questions on hearing the word 'CBI'. A few, like Avni, oozing with curiosity and confidence—though Avni's voice is as tired as the wings of migratory birds—probed further.

Simone says, 'This is regarding the suicides by a few members at the Foundation.'

Silence. Simone hears the sharp boom of an airplane taking off or landing in the background.

'Avni, are you still there?'

'Suicides?' she says, finally.

'Yes. If you don't mind, I'd like to ask you some questions now.'

Silence again. Simone takes it as her cue and asks, 'When did you become a member of the Dream Cancer Foundation?'

'Umm . . . about five-six months ago, shortly after I was diagnosed.'

'With leukaemia?'

'No.' Avni's voice is almost a whisper. 'Clinical depression. I was diagnosed with blood cancer nine months and seventeen days ago. That's 290 days ago. As per the doctor's original prognosis, I have seventy-five days to live.'

Simone raises an eyebrow. It's like Avni is crossing her days down on a calendar with a red marker.

'I'm sorry to hear that,' says Simone.

No response.

'Do you remember Dr Dia Sengupta from the Foundation?'

'Of course. She was the only therapist skilled enough to know what she was talking about. The rest of them were a bunch of brainless, blithering idiots. I attended three, maybe four, group therapy sessions with those clueless moderators. Complete waste of time. Then I attended the session on lucid dreams with Dr Sengupta and I knew if anybody could help me, it was her. I requested a one-on-one session with her. She obliged. Honestly, before I met her, I just wanted to end it. Shoot myself with a gun or something. I still do on most days. But Dr Sengupta helped me manage that deep, powerful urge to hang myself.'

Simone is speechless. She finds it hard to proceed. Not because of Avni's dark intentions, but because when she attempted suicide, it's exactly how she felt—hollow, cold, exhausted—that the only light at the end of the tunnel was the fiery ball of death.

'ASP Singh, are you still there?'

'Yes . . . yes. I'm glad to hear that Dr Sengupta helped you.'

'Yeah, somewhat.'

'Did Dr Sengupta give you a device named Dreamo to help with lucid dreaming?'

'Yes,' Avni says without a pause. 'The device is like magic. Induces lucid dreams like this!' Simone hears Avni snap her fingers.

Simone continues, 'Are you still undergoing therapy with Dr Sengupta?'

'No, not anymore. My parents can't afford her fees. She obliged with two pro bono sessions. Taught me a few techniques that I try to do daily.' Avni scoffs loudly over the phone. 'But it's getting harder to practice the techniques every day, knowing death will find me in seventy-five days, anyway.'

There is utter resignation in Avni's voice. Simone wants to help her, somehow. How?

'Avni, you know that with modern healthcare, most cancer patients outlast their initial prognosis.'

'You are talking about the ones who have the will and the energy to fight on. I'm not one of them.'

Silence.

'Avni, do you know anyone named the Dreamcatcher?'

There is a prolonged silence.

'Avni?'

'Umm . . . sorry, can you repeat that question? I didn't hear you.'

Simone's gut wrenches. She was loud and clear enough. *Why is Avni suddenly cagey?*

'Do you know the Dreamcatch—'

'No, I don't.' Avni responds even before Simone finishes the question.

'Are you sure, Avni? I will check your WhatsApp and Telegram contacts later, and I will know if you are lying.'

Simone plays a gamble. Telegram doesn't cooperate with the police in most countries, including India. There is no way Simone can check Avni's Telegram contacts. But Avni doesn't need to know that. And even if she does, Simone, a credible CBI officer, has now planted doubt in a teenager's naïve mind. It's Avni's call now. She needs to call the bluff or fold.

Simone can hear Avni breathing over the phone. Her breaths are heavy, furious.

'Avni?'

'Yes, yes. Okay? Yes, I know about the Dreamcatcher.'

26

The CBI headquarters is a swanky, new eleven-storey glass building nestled amidst and in stark contrast to the sandstone labyrinth of government ministerial offices built during the British Raj. The old and new, together. It's a government building that is not so *sarkari*. The glass façade is modelled after the Interpol headquarters in Lyon, France—a striking reminder of the European influence in our culture and psyche to this day.

The top brass of CBI sits on the tenth and eleventh floor, giving them a bird's-eye view of the green vistas surrounding Lodhi Road. Simone stands against a conference room window on the fourth floor, chewing the end of a pencil, tapping her feet on the white-marble floor, watching haggard colleagues gather around a ganna *thela* in front of the building. It's forty-five degrees on the streets. Simone smacks her lips, recalling the sweet, refreshing taste of sugarcane juice gushing inside her throat, cooling down every pore it washes over. Grandma used to make sugarcane juice at home every summer. *Used to.*

Simone turns away from the window. 'Are we ready?' she asks Lucas.

Lucas is having an animated discussion with a technician, debating the position of the camera angle. He peels away for a quick second. 'Five more minutes,' he says and goes back to the wrangle with the technician.

Today is sting operation day. Today they nab the Dreamcatcher in the act. Code name: Operation *Catcher in the Rye*. Lucas came up with the code name. He's a self-confessed bookaholic—that's how he has described himself to Simone. At first, she didn't understand what the famous book, *The Catcher in the Rye*, has to do with apprehending the Dreamcatcher. Lucas had explained that 'Like Holden, the protagonist in the book, we are saving kids from falling off a cliff. We, the police, are the catchers in the rye, get it?' Lucas had reasoned with much fanfare and enthusiasm. Simone still doesn't get it, but she lets it pass. She has more pressing matters to think about and argue about. Like keeping Avni alive.

It's been a week since Avni confessed to her friendship with the Dreamcatcher. Avni is suicidal, her mental state a complete mess. She wants to end her life before cancer consumes it anyway in seventy-five days. She confessed she befriended the Dreamcatcher about a month ago. The Dreamcatcher has promised her painless death in her sleep. Today, in ten minutes, exactly at 5 p.m., the Dreamcatcher will call Avni to keep his promise.

Simone and Lucas are prepared. The plan is simple: the Dreamcatcher calls Avni on Telegram, Avni pretends to lucid dream while two CBI personnel and Avni's parents watch over her at their home in Guwahati—ensuring she doesn't kill herself—giving Simone and her tech team in Delhi enough time to trace the call and get the Dreamcatcher's live location. Easy-peasy. The hard part was convincing Avni's parents. They had vehemently opposed the sting operation. No way they were testing their daughter's fragile mental state to nab the supposed killer. Simone had persisted. They finally gave in after Simone told them about her own suicide attempt. It was Lucas's idea. 'People make emotional, not rational decisions,' Lucas had told Simone. 'Tell them your story and they'll trust you.' Lucas was right.

'Where the hell is the voice expert?' Simone hollers. She checks her wristwatch. 'He was supposed to be here by 4.30 p.m.'

'He called.' Lucas looks up. 'He'll be here in ten minutes.'

'The call starts in ten minutes!' fumes Simone. 'Please call him and ask him to get his ass down here right now!'

Lucas nods, pulls out his phone, and scurries out of the room as if the building is on fire.

Simone paces the length of the conference room. *Why can't people be on time?* She has hired a voice expert—a specialist in vocal analysis—because Dia is still their prime suspect, their only suspect. However, Avni confirmed what Noor had stated—the Dreamcatcher is a man with a rich baritone, which reduces Dia's chances of conviction. None of the hundred-odd people they've interviewed so far have a baritone. Simone suspects that the Dreamcatcher alters the voice during the call to hide his identity. Now, the voice expert must ascertain if the Dreamcatcher has tampered with his—or her—actual voice.

'The voice expert is on his way.' Lucas strides back into the room. 'Five minutes out.'

Simone stares at Lucas, doesn't stop pacing.

'We are ready, ma'am,' a technician tells Simone.

Simone looks up at the giant projector screen in front of the room and sees the live feed of the Basumatarys' modest, no-frills living room. Avni is lounging on a sofa, treating herself to a bag of potato chips. Her parents sit beside her, tense and grim, their hands folded, their lips pressed together. Raj and Atirek—her two trusted CBI officers in Guwahati—stand on either side of the parents.

The technician points to a device in the middle of the long, narrow conference room table. 'You will hear the phone conversation between Avni and the perp on this speaker. It's for one-way communication only. You can't speak into it.' He points to another smaller device in front of Simone. 'Use this speaker to address the CBI officers in Guwahati.'

Simone unmutes the speaker. 'Raj and Atirek, do you copy?'

She sees the two officers touch their earpieces on the giant projector.

'Yes, copy,' they both say in unison.

Simone nods. 'Please ask Avni to check her Telegram chats. See if the Dreamcatcher has messaged.'

Atirek passes on the message.

She sees Avni shake her head on the screen. 'Ask Simone ma'am to chill. I'll get a notification when he messages.' Avni bites into a chip.

'Did you hear that, Simone?' says Atirek.

Simone bites her lip. 'Yes, I did.' She mutes the speaker. Simone clenches and unclenches her fingers, trying to rein in her nerves.

The conference room door cracks open, and a young man pushes his head through the little space between the door and its jamb. He is in his late twenties, wearing fluorescent red glasses, and hair coiffed into pointy spikes with a generous dose of hair gel. 'May I come in?' he asks.

'Sorry, who are you?' asks Lucas.

The young man walks in like he owns the place, laptop in hand, and a smirk plastered on his face. He wears tattered jeans and a t-shirt that reads: *I AM NOT YELLING. This is my coach voice.*

'I'm voice coach Sid Reddy.' He stands tall and extends his hand.

Lucas shakes his hand. 'Ah, yes! Finally, you are here.'

'Thank you for waiting. I got stuck in traffic,' says Sid with the confidence of a bullfighter, his chest puffed.

Simone is aghast. *Thank you for waiting?* No apology, no sorry. *Who the hell does he think he is?*

'Yes, of course, it's the traffic to blame, not you,' says Simone.

Sid appraises Simone from top to bottom. His roving eyes make Simone uneasy. He walks over and extends his hand. 'And you are?'

'I am the one who hired you,' Simone says with a prickle of annoyance and stares at him. Then, after a moment, she shakes his hand. His hand is cold, soft and damp, like touching raw bread dough.

What made me hire this blabbering dimwit in the first place? Google reviews, strong credentials and lack of other options at short notice, she recalls.

The smirk on Sid's face widens into a grin. 'I'm voice coach Sid Reddy. At your service, ma'am.' He takes a theatrical bow.

Simone rolls her eyes. 'I heard you the first time, Mr Reddy. You have two minutes. Please setup ASAP,' she says, pushes past him and flops down on a swivel chair.

'Wonderful! I only need one minute,' Sid announces to the room.

He pulls out the chair next to Simone, perches his laptop onto the table, and sits down. 'Now, all I need is a recording of the call.'

Simone asks the technician. 'Can you patch through the live recording of the telephonic conversation with Mr Reddy, please?'

The technician nods.

Sid turns to Simone. 'Thank you, Miss . . . Mrs . . .' He stops. He doesn't know her name.

'No Miss. No Mrs ASP Simone Singh.'

'What does ASP mean?'

Is this guy for real? Simone wants to punch him in the face. She does the next best thing—she swivels her chair and looks away at the screen.

There is a sudden commotion on the screen. Avni jumps up from the sofa, crumples the empty bag of potato chips and throws it on the centre table. She taps her phone screen with renewed vigour.

'We are a go! We are a go!' Atirek's voice booms on the conference room speaker. 'The Dreamcatcher just messaged.'

'Look sharp people,' orders Simone.

They hear a phone ringing on the speaker in the middle of the table. The Dreamcatcher is calling Avni.

Simone sees Avni press the phone against her ears on the screen.

'Avni.' The speaker reverberates with the Dreamcatcher's stentorian voice. The single word rings ominously in Simone's ears. She can't help but think of Amitabh Bachchan enunciating his words in a scene from a Bollywood film.

'Hel . . . hello,' Avni replies.

'Are you ready to sleep, Avni?'

Avni sits back down on the sofa. 'Yes,' she says.

Simone recognizes the surety, the absolute certainty in Avni's voice when she first came clean about her suicidal intentions. She shudders. If they hadn't intervened, Avni would have walked off a cliff on her own.

'We have a trace on the call,' says the technician.

'Wow! Already?' exclaims Sid. 'Never knew that the police worked with such agility in our country.'

Simone shakes her head. Contrary to popular belief— built over many years by crime dramas and movies—call tracing with digital systems is almost immediate. It has been so for decades since we stopped using analogue phones. The police officer whispering in movies—*keep him on the line while we run a trace*—is sheer nonsense.

Simone ignores Sid's snarky comment and asks the technician, 'Show me the location.'

'Oh!' voices the technician.

'What?'

'It's coming from here, in Delhi.'

The projector screen switches to a map of Delhi. A single red dot is flickering on a location in central Delhi.

'Zoom in. And switch to street-view,' says Simone.

The map zooms in and points to a single red-brick house. 'The call is coming from a bungalow in Lutyens Zone.'

Simone stops breathing for a second. The shock is like ice water on her skin.

'The house address is—'

'I know this bungalow.' Simone interrupts the technician. 'It's Dr Dia Sengupta's.'

27

**Audio Journal of *THE DREAMCATCHER*
Audio File #7**

Woohoo! It's Monday, 28 June! I'm so sooo excited!

I know, I know. How can Monday be so exciting? Monday blues, right?

Well, today is Pride Day! Today, I can march on the streets, hand-in-hand with people like me, people who understand me, people who are different and queer, people who have long been shunned and choked and persecuted, today we stand together, today we shout, 'Love is love!' at whoever needs to hear it, whoever deserves it, whoever needs an ally. We stand together in love, dignity and mutual respect. We are a rainbow. And

I am mighty proud to be a part of this luminous, pellucid rainbow.

I have my flag ready for the Pride Parade. I designed and crafted it at home. Okay, I may have copied the design from an Insta video, but hey, I did it myself. It's a starched khaki fabric, brilliant in all colours of the rainbow, with tiny little red hearts, hand-drawn, sprinkled all over. And written across the flag, in neat calligraphy, is a single word, SONALI, my love, my heart, all of it!

Last year, we marched together, Sonali and I, wearing matching crisscross halter tops, hot pink with contrasting orange lace embroidery. At the end of the march, we kissed, our fingers intertwined, lips locked and hearts fused. Time stopped for that moment. We weren't hiding our love. We weren't afraid. We were lesbians in love.

I'll miss you at the Pride Parade this year, Sonali. But know that I have your name scrawled across my flag and my heart.

Miss you, always.

28

Simone turns to Sid, the voice analyst. 'Can you tell me if the caller changed their voice?'

Sid pushes up his glasses. 'I need more time to run the recording through the software for analysis.'

Simone chews her lower lip. She wants to catch Dia in the act. Every second she waits is a second lost.

She decides quickly and speaks into the microphone to the CBI officers in Guwahati. 'Atirek and Raj, we have traced the Dreamcatcher to a location in central Delhi. It's a ten-minute drive from the CBI headquarters. Please keep Avni on the call with the Dreamcatcher. I want to catch him . . . her . . . red-handed. If the call ends early for whatever reason, call me immediately on my mobile phone.'

She doesn't wait for a response.

'Sid,' she says and scribbles rapidly on a Post-it. 'Here's my number. Call me once your analysis is complete. It's urgent.'

'You are leaving?' asks Sid.

She doesn't reply.

'Lucas,' she says, rushing out of the conference room, 'you are coming with me. We have an arrest to make.'

* * *

Simone slams on the accelerator. Her compact four-wheel-drive Mahindra Thar responds immediately, lurching forward with a jolt. The warm evening breeze rushes in through the open window.

'I knew it!' she says aloud. 'The clues were pointing to Dia all along. A trained hypnotist, a practitioner of lucid dreaming—who else could it be? She bought those Dreamo devices, distributed them to her potential victims, and planted them in the *Dream Boxes*. It was a perfect charade—a volunteer for non-profit, free therapy sessions to gain the trust of terminally ill teens struggling with depression, while she intended to murder them, euthanize them, all along. Now we have concrete proof to put her behind bars.'

'Do we?' asks Lucas.

Simone grips the steering wheel tightly. 'What do you mean?'

'I mean, can we arrest her without a warrant?'

'You tell me. You are the one with the photographic memory.'

'I understand what you are referring to. The Code of Criminal Procedure, CrPC, Section 41. Any police officer may without an order from a Magistrate and a warrant, arrest any person against whom a reasonable complaint has been made, or credible information has been received, or a reasonable suspicion exists, of his—'

Simone interrupts. 'So, we can arrest her. No warrant, no red tape, no hassle.'

'Yes, but only for questioning. I don't think a call trace is a concrete proof [he makes air quotes] to charge her with murder. Think about the political frenzy that we'd be stoking. She's the daughter of a cabinet minister, for God's sake.'

It baffles Simone. She flicks her head. 'Are you serious?'

'Humour me,' he says. 'There is no proof that it was her. It could have been anyone. It's circumstantial evidence. If the Dreamcatcher is smart enough to scrub his phone remotely after murdering his victims, he's smart enough to re-route the trace on his call. He is tricking us into thinking it's Dia.'

'Her.'

'Sorry?'

'Not him, *her*. The Dreamcatcher is a woman. It's Dia.'

'Ok, her. Maybe the Dreamcatcher is a woman. But we can't be sure it's Dia.'

Simone shakes her head. She is bristling, anger bubbling; an eruption is just around the corner. *Why is Lucas siding with Dia?*

'Oh, I get it,' she says after a moment as it suddenly strikes her.

'Get what?'

'I told you to keep it professional, Lucas. Didn't I?'

'What are you talking about?'

'Your puppy dog crush on Dia. I saw it. I was there. The way you were making a fool of yourself the last time we visited her. Don't let her fool you now.'

'Are you questioning my integrity, Simone?'

'Yes, I am. You are thinking with your dick, not your head.'

'That's it! Stop the car,' Lucas hisses.

'What? Did I break your little boy heart? Or hurt your tiny little ego?'

'Stop the car. Please.'

'You are on duty, Lucas. If I stop the car and let you out, you'll be defying a direct order from a superior.'

Silence. Lucas purses his lips.

'We are arresting Dia on suspicion of murder. We'll see whether or not the charge sticks.'

Lucas stays mum.

Simone glances at him. 'You are not going to speak now, are you?'

No response.

'Fine. Have it your way.'

Simone swerves abruptly, slams the brakes, and stops the car on the road shoulder.

'Get out, Lucas. I'm giving you a direct order.'

Lucas unlocks the door. 'Thank you,' he murmurs, steps out of the Jeep, and slams the door behind him.

In the ensuing silence, Simone can hear herself seething, her breathing intense, her heart racing.

Suddenly, her phone rings. It's an unknown number.

'Hello!' she barks into the phone.

'Hello, Madame Simone,' says a man, his voice smooth and confident.

'Who is this?'

'It's voice coach Sid Reddy.'

'What did you find?' Simone comes to the point.

'I have the results of the analysis. Based on the spatiotemporal features of the electrical network frequency—ENF—and the variation of time series in—'

'Yes, or no?' Simone snarls. *Why did I hire this moron?* She asks herself, not for the first time today.

'Yes, the original voice is altered with software. There is a significant variation to conclude—'

'Thank you for your service, Sid.' Simone disconnects the call and throws her phone on the empty passenger seat beside her.

She puts the Jeep in gear, clamps on the accelerator and speeds away.

* * *

Simone enters Lutyens' Zone and brings the Jeep to a halt outside the red-brick bungalow. She grabs her phone, jumps out, and marches to the front gate.

'Good evening, madam ji.' The constable on sentry duty pulls up his mask and salutes her.

'Open the gate.'

'Do you have an appointment with minister sahib?'

'I'm here to see Dr Dia.'

'Do you have an appointment?' he repeats.

'No. It's an urgent CBI matter. Open the gate.'

'Okay, let me call Dia ma'am, and ask her.'

'No, don't call her!' She raises her voice, without meaning to.

The constable gives her a quizzical look. 'Sorry, I can't let you in without permission.'

Simone's mind goes into overdrive. *What can she say to make this sentry let her in?*

'I have a warrant for Dr Dia,' she lies. She didn't want to. It goes against her life principles. But she was desperate to get in, desperate to catch Dia, desperate to close this case and prove to everyone that she wasn't an immature, volatile police officer who tried to kill herself. She doesn't want their sympathy, pity or compassion. She wants to prove, once and for all, that she is capable, fierce and worth her title.

'A warrant? Why? What has she done?'

'It's confidential. I cannot tell you. You need to let me enter.'

The constable sighs. He is thinking, deciding. Finally, he says, 'Can I see the warrant, please?'

Shit! He called her bluff.

'No, you may not,' she says with a straight face.

He narrows his eyes. 'I'm sorry, madam ji. Then, I cannot let you in.'

Simone seethes, her temper boiling. She cannot catch Dia red-handed if Dia knows the police are here.

'Okay, call Dia.' She gives in. 'Tell her that ASP Simone Singh is here on an urgent matter. I need to see her. Now!'

The constable nods. He walks back to the makeshift shed, a wooden outhouse to provide a respite from rain and shine, picks up an ancient-looking wired phone and makes the call. He keeps an eye on Simone while he speaks on the phone, as if he half expects her to jump over the front gate without permission.

Simone waits, restless.

The constable returns with a register and a pen. 'You may go in, madam ji. Please add an entry here.' He points to a spot in the register.

Simone is surprised. She was expecting Dia to make her wait—a delay tactic to buy some time. Makes no difference, thinks Simone. She has Dia on the trace, proof enough to make the arrest.

Simone scribbles hurriedly in the register, says a quick 'thank you!' and dashes inside the front gate.

Radhika, Dia's assistant—Simone has met her thrice now—is waiting for her at the main door.

'Good to see you again, Miss Simone,' she says in lucid English with a bright smile. 'This way, please.' She ushers Simone into the foyer.

Simone's phone rings. It's Sub-Inspector Atirek from Guwahati.

'Give me a minute,' she tells Radhika and steps back out.

'Speak,' she barks into the phone.

'Ma'am, I'm calling to let you know that the Dreamcatcher just ended the call. It was abrupt. Think she smelled something fishy. It was in the middle of the dream. Avni was—'

Fuck! Simone closes her eyes. She disconnects the call. Lucas was wrong. Nobody is trying to frame Dia. She is certain now. It's Dia. She is the Dreamcatcher. The sentry at the main gate must have alerted her when he called. That is why she probably unexpectedly ended the call with Avni.

Simone takes a deep breath, gathering strength. This ends today. Suddenly, she is filled with immense fury and renewed vigour. The Dreamcatcher's sway over young, gullible girls ends today. Enough is enough.

Simone marches inside the foyer.

Radhika is waiting for her. She says, 'Dia ma'am is in her office with a patient. Please take a seat while she—'

Simone doesn't pay heed and brushes past Radhika. Nothing can stop her now. She strides to Dia's office, her hard boots clacking against the hardwood floor. She doesn't knock on the door and flings it open.

There, rocking on the armchair, is Dia, the ever-present, fake smile plastered on her face. Like always, she is impeccably dressed—today in a black chiffon saree with a black lace border matching the colour of her heart, thinks Simone.

'Sorry, Simone. Can you wait outside for five minutes, please? I'm with a patient,' says Dia, her voice even, emotionless.

No, this ends now.

'Ms Dia Sengupta, you are under arrest—' Simone stops mid-sentence as she hears soft sobs coming from the sofa.

Simone swivels on her feet. There is indeed someone else in the room. Sitting on the three-seater sofa—the one

Simone has always found uncomfortable—is Noor, the victim who survived. Noor's eyes are bloodshot. Tears roll down her cheeks unchecked. She is dabbing a tissue around her eyes.

'Noor?' Simone murmurs.

Noor averts her eyes.

'Under arrest?' Dia shoots up from the armchair. 'Is this some kind of joke?'

Simone is too bewildered to say anything. She stands still, mouth agape, eyes unblinking. *Is Dia telling the truth? Was she in a therapy session with Noor?* It certainly seems like it. *But then, what about the call trace?* It specifically pointed to this bungalow.

She has come too far to back out now, Simone decides.

'Drop the charade.' Simone glares at Dia. 'I'm arresting you.'

'What's happening, Simone?' asks Noor, in-between sobs. 'Why are you arresting Dr Sengupta?'

'For the suspicion of aiding and abetting the murder of six of her patients.'

'But . . . but . . .' Dia is at a sudden loss for words. 'We discussed it at length the last time, Simone. I didn't murder my patients. All I did was help them.'

Simone pulls out handcuffs. 'We traced a live call with the killer to your house. This bungalow.'

'A live call? When?'

'Till five minutes ago, when your security guard called and alerted you.' Simone walks over to Dia, handcuffs dangling in her hand. 'Please turn around.'

'You are mistaken, Simone. I have been in a therapy session with Noor for the last forty-five minutes. You can ask her.' Dia peers at Noor with pleading eyes. 'Tell her, Noor, tell her!'

Noor sniffles. She has stopped crying now. Confusion has replaced the deep sorrow on her face. 'Dr Sengupta is telling the truth. She was here with me the entire time.'

Damn it! Simone bites the insides of her cheeks. Dia has an alibi, a witness—Noor. She will defend her in the court of law . . . unless Simone breaks Dia and makes her confess.

She has come too far. No stopping now. Simone turns Dia around and cuffs her.

'I didn't do it, Simone. I didn't kill anyone. I swear!' Dia sounds defeated and hapless.

'Save your oaths for the court, Ms Sengupta,' Simone snarls. She shoves Dia from behind. 'Let's go.'

'Radhika!' says Dia to her assistant who is standing by the door now. 'Call father. Call Baiju uncle. Tell them what happened.'

It dawns on Simone that she has intentionally and violently kicked a hornet's nest. An enormous political nest. Dia's father is a cabinet minister. 'Baiju uncle' is Kiran Baiju, the Minister of Law and Justice of India.

'Stop now, Simone,' Dia hisses. 'Or, I promise, this will be the end of your career.'

29

The clock is ticking. Simone has twenty-four hours to produce Dia before a magistrate as per Indian law because the arrest was made without a warrant. Twenty-four hours to force a confession. In twenty-four hours, Simone will either be congratulated by her boss and hailed in newspapers across the country or culled from the CBI and shunned by the IPS. It boils down to Dia's confession. It's all or nothing. She has to—she must—break Dia. Without a confession, Dia will get off scot-free.

But with the impending political maelstrom, Simone has an hour, maybe two, before the full force of the Indian political and justice systems come down hard on her, like a swatter thwacking a housefly. She'll be forced to go to the magistrate tonight, resign later and then profusely apologize. She, unfortunately, has no better social ranking than a pesky housefly.

Unless she gets a confession.

Simone watches Dia sitting alone in the interrogation room, quiet and calm, her arms crossed, her brow furrowed. The glass is transparent, both ways, unlike the interrogation rooms shown in Hollywood crime dramas. The CBI mostly investigates white-collar crimes in India, dealing with high-ranking bank officials, ministers or company executives. There is no need for one-sided glass. The intent, in fact, is the opposite—for all and sundry to ogle at 'famous' people cornered in a cage, their crimes now public. It hurts their egos, they become restless and that makes them contradict themselves during the interrogation.

Simone, however, is dealing with a white-collar serial killer. Perhaps, even a psychopath who is a master hypnotist herself. Simone has to best Dia at mind games, lay a minefield of traps and let Dia trip over with contradicting facts.

Simone's phone rings. It's SP Vijesh Jaiswal, her boss. *Shit! He knows.* If she answers the phone, she'll be asked to stop and release Dia without prejudice. It does not matter whether she answers the call now or later; she will face the consequences. Later is better. Later gives her time to break Dia. Simone ignores the call. She puts her phone on airplane mode, pockets it, and strides into the interrogation room.

Simone flings the door open. The door swings with force and hits the wall hard. *Bang!* It is intentional, done to elicit a response.

Dia stays calm and composed.

Simone pulls out a chair. The irksome sound of chair legs scraping on the uncarpeted floor fills the room.

No response. Dia gazes at Simone with quiet understanding, like a tolerant mother looks at a toddler throwing temper tantrums.

'You seem nervous, Simone. Are you okay?'

Simone bites her lower lip. There it is—the first punch, the first stab of mind games.

Simone sits down, her back against the door. 'Can I get you some water or coffee?' she asks a feeble attempt to counter Dia and match her composure.

'No, I am very comfortable. Thank you for asking.' Dia sits back and clasps her hands together in her lap.

'Let's get to the facts—'

'Sorry to interrupt you,' says Dia. 'I'm expecting a call from my lawyer. Will you be a peach and let me know when he calls?'

Simone's cheeks must have turned crimson because she feels the heat rising to them. She grips and mushes the arms of her chair to control herself.

'The facts are clear.' Simone decides to ignore Dia. 'We have proof that you bought Dreamo devices and used them to murder six girls.'

'You don't have any proof because I didn't do it. Come on, you are smarter than that, Simone.' Dia shakes her head. 'I bought atta, doesn't mean I made rotis.'

The truth of that sentence burns into Simone.

'We traced a live call to your house, a call where you, the Dreamcatcher, were remotely hypnotizing a young, gullible girl.'

'Then either the tracer was faulty, or someone is trying to frame me.'

'The fact is—'

'The fact is that you arrested me without cause. You are desperate, Simone. Desperate to make it a murder case when, in fact, your victims committed suicide. Desperate to prove that you are mentally fit after you gulped down sleeping pills to kill yourself. I understand. I'm your therapist. I feel your pain. Your grandma just died. Your only family, your only friend. You must feel—how do I put it delicately—quite inadequate.'

Simone stiffens. A deluge of emotions falls onto her. She is suffocating in the interrogation room. The tables have turned. Dia, her therapist, is grilling her, torturing her with the truth—the truth that Simone had revealed to her in confidence.

Simone pulls herself together, like trying to put together broken shards of glass with Sellotape. 'The call came from your bungalow. The call tracer is never wrong.'

'You are a detective, right? Then you must solve the mystery of the defective tracer.'

Simone grinds her teeth. 'It was you. I know it was you.'

'Repeating it won't make it true. I didn't do it. I didn't kill anyone. Plain and simple.'

A silence ensues as they both stare at each other.

'I'm afraid your time's up, Simone.'

Simone narrows her eyes. 'Oh, don't you worry. I have the entire night to get the truth out of you.'

Dia tilts her head and smiles. 'No, you don't.' She nudges her head, gesturing to something behind Simone.

Simone twists in her seat.

A squad of four lawyers, dressed in black open-breasted coats, white-collared shirts, and white bands with gowns, march towards the room. Leading the pack of lawyers is SP Vijesh Jaiswal.

Shit! Simone sighs. Her time is up—in more ways than one.

'Simone . . .' Dia gets up from her seat. 'I hope you don't try to kill yourself again after this embarrassment. I, for one, won't be there to help you.'

Before Simone can muster a reply, the door flings open and SP Jaiswal storms in. 'This interview is over,' he says.

30

Simone taps her feet on the marble floor outside SP Vijesh Jaiswal's office. She is restless, waiting for judgment. SP Jaiswal is in conference with the director general of the CBI, the big boss, and his coterie of advisers. Simone's actions have brought the CBI brass together. Currently, they are interrogating Lucas to get a lowdown on how the shit hit the fan so quickly and so spectacularly.

Simone will be called in next. She feels like a primary school kid who is sent to the principal's office for colouring outside the box. Simone checks her watch. 9.40 p.m. As if on cue, her stomach growls. She looks around sheepishly. The corridor is empty. Nobody heard her stomach rumble. She skipped lunch as she was nervous about the sting operation to catch the Dreamcatcher. She skipped dinner, hoping to crack Dia. But food is the last thing on her mind. One, and only one, question plagues her mind: *why was I so convinced that Dia is the Dreamcatcher?* The answer eludes her.

Dia was not produced before a magistrate. She was not charged with murder. Instead, SP Jaiswal had apologized to Dia profusely and sent her home with a police escort. He hasn't spoken a single word to Simone since he stormed the interrogation room.

The door opens. Lucas steps out of the room and closes the door behind him. He glares at Simone. She averts her gaze.

He comes and sits next to Simone. He stretches his neck and sighs aloud. Simone continues to look at the wavy striations of the marble floor.

'You are in deep trouble, Simone.'

'You think I don't know that?'

Silence.

'Then why did you do it? We both knew the evidence was circumstantial. I tried to tell you. I tried to stop you. But—'

'Thank you for your concern, Lucas. But I neither need your concern nor your pity.'

Lucas shakes his head. 'You keep acting like this and you'll be left with no friends.'

'I have no friends,' Simone retorts. 'Now, if you are done, can you leave me alone?'

'You know what?' He shoots up from the chair. 'Go to hell, Simone!' He twists on his heels and walks away, his strides long and fast.

Simone watches him leave. Deep down, her heart breaks a little, watching another person in her life walk away from her. It's her own fault, though. Simone knows. She deserves it. She deserves to be alone. She deserves to die. Maybe Dia was right. Sleeping pills didn't do the trick.

But a bullet in the head certainly would. On instinct, her hand clasps the holster carrying her service revolver.

The door opens again.

The director general of the CBI steps out followed by his advisers. Simone stands up and salutes the senior officers. The director general ignores Simone and brushes past her without a word. The other officers follow suit. One frowns and shakes her head as she walks past Simone. Another, a grumpy old joint-director, scowls at Simone as if she was a hardened criminal.

Simone keeps her head held high, her hand locked in a salute position, her face not betraying the upheaval ravaging her insides.

The SP pops his head out of the doorway. 'Simone, come inside.'

Simone drops her hand and follows him inside the room.

'Close the door and take a seat,' he orders.

Simone does as instructed.

SP Jaiswal sits back in his chair, clasps his hands and peers at Simone. He remains quiet, letting the gravity of the situation burden Simone. His face betrays neither emotion nor his age. He is in his early forties but looks younger—mostly because of good eating and fitness habits rather than genetics. But stress spares no one in their line of work, and SP Jaiswal is no exception. Fine lines have sprouted around his eyes, as have white hair in his sideburns.

'Do you know the difference between the CBI and the state police?' he asks.

Many answers spring up in Simone's mind, none reach her lips.

'People trust the CBI,' he answers. 'Over the years, we have built a reputation for honest, excellent police work. The CBI is called when the state police mess up. Or, when the case is complex. Or, when prominent citizens of our country indulge in unfathomable crimes. We are trusted to solve those cases—with integrity, diligence and excellence.'

He pauses so that the words can settle.

'Today, that trust was tarnished. Today, we lost face. While the top brass holds you responsible, I believe the fault is mine. I trusted you too much, too early. I pushed you, thinking you are mentally fit for a high-profile case. I thought it'd do you good. I thought it'll help you bounce back from . . . you know . . .'

He gestures with his hand, as if referring to a shared secret he doesn't want to say aloud. Simone knows what he means. It's an open secret: her attempted suicide.

Simone nods. *Get to the point. Tell me if I still have a job or not?*

SP Jaiswal leans back, the swivel chair creaking with the shift in weight. He remains silent, assessing, thinking, deciding. Then he bends forward and says, 'ASP Simone Singh, you are suspended indefinitely.'

Simone exhales. Suspension is better than termination.

SP Jaiswal continues, 'The court-appointed therapist must ascertain and approve the well-being of your mental state before you can recommence police duty.'

There is a complete hush. *This is worse than termination.*

'Please leave your badge and service revolver here. You are free to go.'

Simone doesn't hear the last part. She is stuck on what SP Jaiswal said earlier. *The court-appointed therapist must ascertain her mental state? Shit!* Her court-appointed therapist is Dia. Her career is in Dia's hands. Dia can decide to keep Simone suspended indefinitely.

'Simone, did you hear me?'

Simone comes out of her reverie. She clears her throat. 'Court-appointed therapist? Who?'

SP Jaiswal nods. It's clear.

'Until the court appoints another therapist to manage the conflict of interest—which could be days, weeks even— for now, Dia remains your therapist.'

Simone closes her eyes and murmurs to herself. 'Fuck.'

31

Audio Journal of *THE DREAMCATCHER*
Audio File #8

Phew! That was a narrow escape. For a moment, I thought Simone had figured it out. She came so close! Turns out, she was only shooting in the dark. But I was so scared. I thought I'd be locked in a prison, wearing a grimy white saree for the rest of my life. Worse case, hanged!

Not that I haven't thought of it before. Hanging from a rope, my neck snapped in two, my feet dangling, lifeless. I have. Many times. I knew what I was getting into when I euthanized Sonali. I was aware of the repercussions and consequences. But they don't deter me. I am on a mission. There is a higher purpose—to save those who can't save themselves. I know how they feel. I know how cancer gnaws out every ounce of strength, rendering one helpless, depressed and a burden on their family.

The families know that the best way to treat terminally ill patients is to relieve them from the illness. But they are too close, too attached emotionally. They can't let go. They can't pull the plug even if the patients ask for it. They think a comfortable hospital bed, morphine oozing through the bloodstream and repeated chemotherapy maybe, probably, will save their kin. They don't think of the permanent bed sores or the many needles that prick the skin during cancer treatment. IV medication? Prick. IV fluids? Prick. Blood sample? Prick. Dye injection for a PET scan? Prick. All those pricks and pokes that enmesh our veins. So much so that after a while, there is no space left for a prick.

And for what? A terminally ill patient will die anyway in a few months. Why not save the trouble? Why not reach the same outcome faster?

Trust me, what I do is a relief for them. They want it. They beg for it. I know because I'm one of them. I'm on the same journey. If I don't help them, who will?

32

'Hello,' says Lucas, his voice groggy, the annoyance clear in his tone.

'Umm . . .' Simone has called Lucas to apologize for her behaviour, but now she's suddenly stumped, unsure what to say or where to begin. She adjusts the phone in her hand.

'What do you want, Simone?'

Simone decides the apology can wait. 'Anything new on Dia?' she blurts out.

Lucas sighs over the phone. 'Why are you so obsessed with her? For God's sake, Simone. It's around midnight! I was sleeping. And, not sure if you remember, but you are off the case. Suspended.'

Simone doesn't need another reminder.

'Fine!' Simone raises her voice. 'Go to sleep.' Simone intones the last word as if it were a slur. 'I'll be here at home the whole night, working the case, while you get your beauty sleep.'

'Look,' Lucas clears his throat and says in a composed tone, 'there is not much to work with. Dia has an alibi, a

176

witness. Noor says Dia was in a session with her the entire time the Dreamcatcher was on the call with Avni.'

'Then why did the tracer point to Dia's bungalow?'

'I don't know, Simone. I still think it wasn't Dia. She is being targeted by someone. I don't know who. I don't even know if it's one person or many. They are using Dia's fascination with lucid dreams and the Dreamos she distributed to dupe her and hoodwink us.'

Simone shakes her head. *Lucas and his infatuation with Dia.* She decides not to press him. Instead, she asks, 'Can you send me the recording of the conversation between the Dreamcatcher and Avni? I missed it in the hurry to catch Dia.'

Silence. Lucas is thinking.

'It's against the rules. I can't do that, I'm sorry,' he says finally.

'At least think about it, okay?'

Lucas lets out an audible yawn. 'Simone, I'm too tired to think right now. If you want to work while on suspension, be my guest. But I'm going to sleep.'

'Lucas . . .'

'Yes, what?'

Simone gulps. She closes her eyes. It's tough to admit it. But if not now, then when?

'I'm sorry,' she says.

Silence. Lucas wasn't expecting it.

'I'm sorry about how I behaved with you earlier. I don't know what came over me. I was desperate. I think I still am . . . to close this case. I want to nab the Dreamcatcher and . . .'

'And what?' asks Lucas.

'I don't know why I want it so badly. I love closing cases. Every police officer does. But I don't know why I'm so desperate with this one. I am jumping to conclusions. I am forcing theories. My instincts are taking over my rationality.'

'That's not a bad thing, Simone. Maybe this case is about trusting your instincts, going with the flow, working hand-in-hand with chaos.'

'I don't like chaos. I like control,' mumbles Simone.

Lucas chuckles. 'I know. I've worked with you long enough to know that anything uncontrollable irks your very core.'

For a few moments, nobody speaks. An air of collective camaraderie hangs between them.

'Do you know I have a younger brother?' says Lucas.

'Yes, you told me on the flight to Shillong that you were the eldest of three siblings.'

'Right. My baby brother is ten years younger than me. He's eighteen now. His name is Aaron, named after my dad, who died in a freak accident when my brother was still in the womb. I remember the day mom returned from the hospital and laid Aaron on my lap. He was chubby and pink, swaddled in a baby's blanket, sleeping. I caressed his soft head and promised mom I'd protect him for the rest of his life. He was my responsibility. In dad's absence, even more so.'

Lucas becomes quiet.

Simone waits. She senses there is more to the story.

'I lied to you earlier,' says Lucas. 'I am tired, but I wouldn't be able to sleep. I can't sleep because Aaron hasn't returned home. Every night I lay awake in bed, worried and restless, till he returns, drunk and out of his senses on most nights. Mom has given up on him. My sister, the middle child, has learned to live with it. I can't.'

Lucas inhales deeply. Simone can tell how hard it is for him to even talk about it.

Lucas continues. 'I have tried everything in my control. Counselled him the first time he came home drunk. Scolded him the second time it happened. Slapped him hard across the face the next time. I only made it worse. And now, I wait for him every night, hoping, praying that he doesn't get hit by a bus on the way home, get shot in a dingy bar or get mugged and stabbed in a rough neighbourhood. Every scenario my mind ends with him dying on the streets, lying in a pool of his own vomit and blood.'

Lucas takes another deep breath.

'I cannot explain the relief that pours over me when Aaron gets home finally. It's funny how I didn't want him to drink and now I'm relieved he comes home drunk, happy he is not dead.'

Simone wants to reach out and hold Lucas's hand, just like he had held hers on the flight to Shillong.

'You know what Aaron said last night as I watched over him while he puked into the toilet bowl?'

'What?' asks Simone.

'He apologized. He said he will try to get it under control. And true to his word, he went to his first Alcoholics

Anonymous meeting today. He sent me a photo from there as proof. I didn't need proof. I didn't ask for it. He still sent it.'

Lucas chuckles.

'Now, he still hasn't returned home. There's a high chance he'll come home drunk again, but I think today will be better than yesterday.'

Simone bobs her head, even though she knows Lucas can't see her. She's happy for Lucas.

'All these years I tried to control him, restrict him, but I made it worse. Now, as I go with the flow, as I relinquish control—though still worried sick, sleepless at night—somehow, I have met him midway. At least, I hope I did.'

'You did, Lucas. You did.'

Lucas sighs. 'I know you are desperate, Simone. I was too. Give it time. Let it unfold. You never know, it might be exactly what you need to crack this case wide open.'

33

Dia stands in her walk-in wardrobe, mesmerized by the brilliant colours of the five hundred-plus designer sarees—mostly silk, georgette, and chiffon—and the dazzling shimmer of the three hundred-odd luxury footwear—mostly stilettos, cone heels, and pumps—that she owns. The sarees are arranged by material first, and then by colour. The footwear is arranged by colour, so it's easy to match with her choice of saree. Built-in spotlights, one above each section of the wardrobe, accentuate every sparkle, every contour of her prized collection. This is her happy place. She comes here when she is missing her mum, like today. It is her death anniversary.

It was her mum's wardrobe, collection—all of it built with painstaking effort and ill-gotten money. As a child, Dia was not allowed inside this walk-in wardrobe. She only saw it—the glittery dreamland—from afar. She wanted to enter it so badly someday. *You want what you cannot have*—her first lesson in psychology. When she turned ten, mum gave her an option to earn her way in by ironing and folding *every* saree in the wardrobe. Dia accepted. Mum counted. 'One cares only for what they sow,' mum used to say. After a year of persistent, disciplined labour, mum allowed Dia inside.

She vividly remembers the day she stepped foot inside this sanctuary. It was also the first day she wore a saree. She could choose any saree, mum told her. She had earned it. That day, standing in front of the mirror, wearing a pink chiffon saree with pearl lacing, her feet snug into daisy-white stilettos that were two sizes too large, she felt like a grown-up.

And when mum died, the wardrobe was all hers. *Died?* She mulls over the word, remembering the last day she saw mum, frail, writhing in pain, reeking on her deathbed, holding onto the last shred of life. Cancer, last stage. The doctors had given up. Father was in a campaign rally. Dia was alone with mum. For weeks, the doctors kept saying it'd be mum's last day. Mum was in pain but too stubborn to die. Dia had to nudge. One tiny little nudge. Mum had already fallen off the cliff; she was mid-air when Dia pushed her to the ground. *Does that make me a murderer?* Nope, she decides, pressing her hands together. *I euthanized; I didn't murder. I helped mum. I put her out of her misery, out of her deep, unfathomable pain.*

Suddenly, she is cold, unnerved by the memory of her own deed. The walls of the walk-in wardrobe close in on her. The dazzle is too bright. Dia flips the lights off and dashes out into her bedroom. She is huffing and trembling, beads of sweat form on her forehead. She raises her quivering hands. The hands that ironed out the wrinkles from mum's sarees, the hands that pressed mum's feet to soothe her, the hands that pulled the plug on mum.

She murdered mum.

No, I euthanized her, she corrects herself.

Deep down, she knows, she believes, she helped mum find peace. It was an act of charity, an act of love. It was what mum wanted.

If you love someone, sometimes it's best to let them go.

34

Simone peels away a thin film of sweat from her forehead and flicks it away. Her shirt is drenched, glued to her back with sweat. She squirms on the uncomfortable three-seater sofa in Dia's office and lets out a loud groan. It seems there is a power outage—no lights, air-conditioning or fan. But the lampposts in the garden outside are lit bright yellow. *Maybe they have a different power source than the rest of the bungalow? Solar?*

She squints at the wall clock in the darkness. The feeble light from the lampposts is just enough to see the clock hands pointing to 8.40 p.m. It's been forty minutes since Radhika, Dia's assistant, showed her in and locked her alone in the hot, dark room. Yes, *locked*. Simone had tried turning the doorknob twenty minutes ago. It didn't budge.

It's a game, Simone knows. Dia is making her wait on purpose. Locking her in the office like Simone had locked her in the interrogation room. Tit for tat. It's Dia's way of exacting revenge. *Well, who'd blame her after the embarrassment she went through?* Simone isn't panicking, though. She has all the time in the world. No job, no family. If not here, she'd be at home doing the same—counting the hours.

And besides, Dia needs to give Simone a clean bill of mental health before the latter joins the police force. Simone gathers her resolve. Dia can throw cheap tricks at her if she likes. She will not break.

Simone hears the unmistakable click of the door unlocking. The door creaks open slowly. Dia stands in the doorway; her gaze locked on Simone, her face expressionless, lit by the candle she has been holding. No fake smile, no unfettered enthusiasm today. Dia looks haggard and mournful as if she's returning from a cremation. Her hair is untied, and she hasn't pinned up the *pallu* of her off-white saree. Her forehead is creased with wrinkles, and she isn't wearing glasses that match the colour of her saree. Something's off . . . something beyond the embarrassment of getting arrested.

Dia enters the room with measured steps, sits on the armchair, and rocks back and forth, the candle in her hand burning bright. Not once does she look away from Simone, like a ghost straight out of a horror movie, silent and unblinking. Simone feels a chill crawl down her sweaty back. She has never liked horror movies. Dia knows it. Simone had disclosed it in a previous session. She thinks Dia is trying to scare her now. It's working. She's shitting bricks.

Simone looks away and starts tapping her feet against the hardwood floor. She is becoming jittery.

Dia places the candle on the side table and picks up the air-con remote. She presses a button, and the air-con vents flutter open with a hiss.

'The remote was right here all along,' says Dia. 'All you had to do was press a button and trust that the power was on.'

Simone stays mum. *Is there a hidden lesson that Dia wants to impart?*

Dia crosses one leg over the other. 'It's the same with depression. The help is right here, Simone.' Dia points to herself. 'But if you aren't willing to pick up the remote or trust the person who is trying to help you, then . . .' She shrugs her shoulders and lets the words hang, their meaning clear.

Silence. They stare at each other for a few seconds.

Fine. Lesson learned. Simone stands up, walks to the light switch panel, and is about to switch the lights on when Dia says, 'Stop. No lights today. We are in mourning. It's my mother's death anniversary. We keep the lights switched off today.'

Simone wants to point to the lit lamp posts in the garden and the hypocrisy in Dia's words, but she pulls back her hand, retraces her steps and sits back down.

'Radhika!' Dia calls out.

Her assistant comes rushing into the room. 'Yes, ma'am?'

'Please bring Simone's medication.'

Medication? Simone wiggles uneasily on the sofa.

Radhika nods and dashes out.

'We need to up the ante, Simone. Tackle your depression head-on. Use every bullet in our arsenal.'

Radhika rushes back in with a small white pill box and hands it to Simone.

Simone hesitates. 'What are these?'

'Sleeping pills. Higher dose than the ones you used to kill yourself,' says Dia, her tone even.

Simone gulps. Dia is tempting her, taunting her to attempt suicide again. A part of her is scared. But a part of her wants to grab the box and empty it in her mouth— right now, right here—and end this psychotic game that Dia is playing.

Instead, Simone grasps the box and twirls it in her hand, the pills rattling inside. She is transfixed by how much power a little box can hold. One pill relaxes, one pack kills. She was lucky to survive the last suicide attempt. But Dia is taking luck out of the equation for the next time.

Dia says, 'You must take one pill every night . . . more if you fancy.' She winks and smiles. 'You must video call me. I want to see you swallow the pill. Every. Single. Night.'

There is unconcealed joy in Dia's words. *She is enjoying it like a deplorable sadist*. She keeps mum, keeps a lid on the anger bubbling inside her.

Dia continues. 'I will review your progress every week. And if, after a year, I deem you mentally fit, I'll recommend you for active police duty.'

'A year!' Simone yelps.

Dia smirks and nods.

Simone says, 'It's unfair and unethical, and you know it!'

Dia stops rocking the armchair, hunches forward. 'Was handcuffing me fair? Was dragging me to the CBI headquarters without a warrant ethical?'

Simone doesn't have an answer. She fidgets, feeling trapped.

A long silence ensues.

'However,' says Dia, simpering. 'There is a faster way.'

Now what?

'I remember you received a letter from your birth mother, who's in Tihar Jail.'

Simone raises her brows.

'I think it'll help you embrace your past and find closure. Maybe even cure your depression faster.'

No! She knows what Dia is hinting at. *No, I can't do it!*

Dia sits back and rocks the armchair. Her smirk broadens into a smile. 'You must visit your birth mother in prison. Listen to what she has to say. And maybe it'll bring you inner peace.'

35

Simone wipes her face with a handkerchief and pockets the now-damp cloth. The serpentine queue outside Tihar Jail nudges forward and Simone trudges underneath the shed at the entrance. Simone raises her head and peers at the royal blue plastic shed curved outwards like a canopy and soldered above crisscrossed iron bars. A large signboard, also royal blue, hangs beneath the shed, announcing in crisp white lettering the entrance to the many jails inside Tihar. Jail Number 6—home to over four hundred female convicts—is among them. One of those women is Simone's birth mother, languishing in a cell for twenty-four years, for murdering her husband.

Why? Simone doesn't want to know. She doesn't want to be here. She doesn't want to meet a cold-blooded killer. Even if it's her mother. To Simone, she is a stranger, like the many others standing in the queue to enter the jail. Nameless strangers she doesn't care about; faceless strangers she wouldn't recognize if she walks past them again on a street.

Why am I doing this? she asks herself, not for the first time today. *Is it about getting my job back?* She has agonized over the question since she met Dia two days ago. *No!* She has concluded. *It's about getting my identity back.* She is a police officer. Period.

'Next!' The prison officer on gatekeeping duty calls out to her.

Simone walks over and says, 'I booked an appointment on the National Prisons Portal to visit Ms Shobha Dogra.' Simone was born into a Dogra family. She assumed the surname *Singh* from her adopted family. She shows the officer a printout of the registration form and her identity proof.

The officer reads the documents. 'ASP?' He immediately salutes Simone. 'Sorry, ma'am, I didn't recognize you without the police uniform.'

Simone acknowledges the salute. She stops herself from explaining why she isn't in uniform. 'I'm with the CBI,' she says instead. CBI officers are not required to wear police uniforms, even though Simone prefers to. It's a better excuse than explaining her suspension.

'CBI officers don't stand in a queue at police premises, ma'am. You should have come directly to me.'

'Rules are rules. Same for everyone,' she says.

The officer chuckles. 'But that doesn't mean we can't bend them a little.'

Before Simone can object, he calls out to a deputy prison officer (DPO) behind him. 'DPO Rathor, please escort ASP Singh to the VIP visitor area of Jail Number 6.'

Rathor salutes Simone and says, 'Please follow me, ma'am.'

Rathor leads Simone through a maze of crumbling brick buildings and pruned gardens. They enter Jail Number 6, a freshly painted structure that stands in stark contrast to the rest of the premises. It's unlike any local jail Simone has visited in her brief career. It's modern, sparkly, clean and painted with a thick coat of white with maroon lining. The best part—it smells of freshly cooked daal-chawal, homely and inviting.

Rathor seems to read Simone's mind. 'The female prison is like a resort for many convicts. There is an environment of sisterhood and harmony here. They get along with each other, and most of them train and aspire to a respectable life once they get out. While the male prison is a hub of extortion rackets, hit jobs and frequent inmate scuffles, we haven't had a major offence in the female prison in the last ten months,' he says with pride.

They enter the central courtyard lined with inmate cells with iron bars for doors. A group of thirty-odd inmates are squatting in the courtyard, huddled together, weaving needles through embroidery hoops. A few give a quick, lazy glance to Simone and go back to stitching.

They walk along the corridor and past a large, noisy room with a half-open wooden door. Simone peeks inside. A group of women are tailoring with intent on sewing machines. Some are chatting, laughing and joking with jail supervisors. Simone nods in appreciation. Rathor was right. Of all the places in the world, she has witnessed a prevailing sense of sisterhood in the sunlit corridors of a jail.

'This way,' says Rathor. He ushers Simone into a room lined with two two-seater sofa sets on the right and a set of two plastic chairs and a rickety desk on the left. 'Would you like to have water or juice, ma'am?'

Simone declines.

'Please make yourself comfortable. Shobha *amma* must be in the kitchen. I'll ask her to meet you here.'

'Amma?' Simone blurts out.

Rathor chuckles. 'That's what we call her lovingly. She's quite a celebrity here. Everybody knows her, and she knows everybody. The officers trust her, the inmates look up to her. She's like our adopted mother here at Tihar.' He pauses. 'How do you know her, by the way? She's never had a visitor . . . until today.'

Simone swallows hard. 'I'd rather not say,' she mumbles.

Rathor presses his lips together and nods. 'I'll bring her,' he says and leaves.

Simone presses her hands together. Despite the heat, an icy chill runs down the small of her back. She is nervous, like a kid on the first day of school. Giddy and intimidated. Jumpy and tense. She was so consumed with the decision of whether to visit at all, but now that she is here, she doesn't know what to say to her mother.

Simone walks to the sofas, bends down and rubs her hand over the sofa seat, dusting it off.

'Don't worry. We clean them every day, bachchu,' says a sweet, calm voice.

Simone stops dusting the sofa and stands upright, frigid in place. *There she is. My mother.* Her heart thumps like an uncontrollable piston.

Shobha amma might be a stranger, but she is her mother. She might not remember her love or her hugs or her kisses, but now, in this moment, staring into her soft, gleaming eyes and radiant, ageing face, Simone is certain she was loved and hugged and kissed by this stranger, her mother . . .

. . . before she killed her husband and gave up Simone for adoption.

And suddenly, Simone finds her birth mother responsible for her tough childhood and for her difficult adolescence. Anger courses through her veins. What if her mother hadn't killed him? What if her mother hadn't given her up? What if? Her mother robbed her of every *what if* that could have been.

Shobha amma limps inside, her right leg unable to support her own weight for long. She is wearing a white cotton *salwar-kameez*, no jewellery except a silver *kada* on her wrist, her hair—more grey than black—is tied in an untidy bun, her brows need generous threading, and her roly-poly face beams with a natural lustre. She is carrying a tiny plastic bowl covered with a paper napkin.

She comes inside and appraises Simone from top to bottom like a mother does on seeing her child after years—proud, happy, content. She raises her hand to touch Simone on the chin but then withdraws it at the last moment.

'The bald look suits you,' she says with a smile.

Simone fidgets awkwardly.

She limps to the sofa and flops down with a thump and a loud sigh of relief. 'Come, sit.' She pats the seat next to her.

Simone chooses to sit on the other sofa.

'I'm glad you came.'

Simone nods but doesn't say a word.

'I wasn't sure if you'd come after I sent the letter. I thought—'

'Why did you send me the letter? Why, after all these years?' Simons asks, her voice filled with accusation.

Shobha amma purses her lips. 'I thought you deserved to know before . . .' She stops herself. She removes the napkin from the plastic bowl. 'I brought you some halwa. I cooked it myself. Only for you.' She beams.

'I don't eat sweets,' says Simone.

Shobha amma swallows hard and puts the napkin back over the bowl.

'I deserve to know what?' asks Simone.

'You deserve to know why I killed your father. Why am I still here when I could have paroled out years ago? Why did I reach out to my only daughter after all these years?'

'Had,' says Simone bluntly. 'You had a daughter. You gave her up for adoption.'

Silence.

After a while, Shobha amma says, 'You used to love sweets when you were very young. Like any other kid, I guess. Do you know which food you tasted first?'

Simone shrugs her shoulders.

'Honey.' She is beaming again. 'I put a few drops of honey on my little finger—your *nani* had brought it to the hospital—and I inserted the finger in your mouth. You loved it! You sucked my finger with such gusto that the nurses at the next station stopped working on hearing you click your tongue.' She smiles reminiscing about the memory.

Simone is unmoved. She doesn't remember. It isn't her memory, even though she was there.

'But your *dadi* frowned upon it. She thought it was unsanitary. Told your dad all about it.' She pauses, her face grim. 'Do you know what your dad did when I reached home carrying you from the hospital?'

No response.

'He grabbed me by the throat, pulled back my hair, inserted two fingers smeared with red chili in my mouth and forced me to suck them. He stopped only after I vomited. Then he took out his belt. I had vomited on him after all. I had to bear the consequences.'

Pin drop silence.

'He wanted to teach me a lesson. It wasn't the first time. It wasn't the last. But I remember it most vividly because that man spoiled my first memory of *you*, my daughter. Now, I can't think of honey without thinking of red chilli.'

Simone bites her lower lip. *My mother has been a victim of domestic violence?* A part of her softens up. If a man abused Simone, she'd beat him black and blue.

'I didn't kill him then. For three years, I was married to that devil. I didn't kill him when he punched me or belted me, or raped me. He broke my leg with an iron rod and left me with a limp, but I didn't kill him. I didn't kill him after he poured kerosene on me and tried to burn me alive.'

She pauses and inhales deeply. 'His mother snatched the lighter from him at the last moment. The only thing I am grateful for to your dadi.' She shakes her head. 'No, I didn't kill him then.'

She looks up at Simone. There is a fire, a certain ferocity in her eyes. She says, 'I killed him—no, I hacked him to pieces—after he stubbed a burning cigarette on your cheek when you wouldn't stop crying one night.'

She points to the mark on Simone's right cheek. Simone has always thought it to be a birthmark. Uneven tone, no big deal. *No. It's a scar. It is a big deal.*

'There. Now you know the short version of why I'm here. But I didn't tell you this to get your sympathy or your kindness or rekindle a relationship that was never built.' She pauses. 'Before I leave, I wanted you to understand why a mother would give up her daughter, why I gave you up—to keep you safe.'

'Leave? Are you getting out of jail?'

Shobha amma chuckles. 'My sweet bachchu, I am dying. I am leaving . . . life. Soon.'

Simone is imbued with a deep sorrow that fills up the void. Her heart aches and hands tremble. 'Brilliant! Just brilliant, isn't it?' She shoots up from the sofa and raises her voice. 'Just when I find family, I lose them. The story of my fucking life!'

A lump forms in her throat. Her mouth twists as she tries not to cry. She came here to talk to a stranger. But now, she wants this stranger in her life. She wants a mother. She wants a family.

Shobha amma gets up from the sofa and limps over to Simone. 'Come here,' she says.

'No, don't touch me.' Simone warns.

Shobha amma ignores Simone, grasps her shoulders and pulls her into a bear hug. Simone tries to push her away, but she is surprisingly strong.

'Oh, *mere* bachchu . . .' She rubs Simone's back with one hand.

Simone stops struggling. The lump in her throat burns. She lets out a deep-throated gurgle, and suddenly, tears flow down her cheeks in an unchecked stream. Simone bawls, screams and lets her pain out. The pain she has hidden all her life. But today, without warning, the dam has burst open.

They stand hugging each other for a long time. Simone's cries turn into sniffles. Shobha amma's smile turns into sobs.

'Come,' Shobha amma says and nudges Simone to sit down. 'Here, try my sooji halwa. Everyone here says I'm an excellent chef. You know, I've written two recipe books also?' she says with pride.

Simone smiles.

'Try the halwa and tell me if it's any good.'

Simone dips her fingers into the warm, rich dessert and puts a small morsel into her mouth. Her eyes close as the soft, sumptuous halwa melts, enamouring all her taste buds with delectable flavours.

Maybe Dia was right. After struggling for months with depression, here—sitting next to her mother, revelling in the aftertaste of sooji halwa—Simone feels sunrays pierce through the grey cloud that has been hovering over her head, dissolving it into vapours, like it was never there.

She has found her happy place.

36

Avni marks a bold X with a red marker on today's date on her bedside calendar. She has sixty days to live. At least, according to the original prognosis when the doctor told her she has leukaemia. Incurable.

She could have died a painless death had the police not interrupted her well-laid plans. Avni is no longer in touch with the Dreamcatcher. Her parents have taken away her phone. They don't trust her anymore. Avni is no longer alone, ever. Her parents keep a twenty-four-hour vigil. She can't talk to friends without her mother eavesdropping. She has strict instructions not to lock the bathroom door from inside. Whenever she uses the bathroom, her paranoid mother stands guard outside, and pops her head in every few minutes, making sure Avni is relieving and not killing herself. Her mother even sleeps with her now!

Argh! Am I a kid?

If anything, her desire for suicide has only intensified. Her life has gone from a struggle to miserable to unliveable. She's done with it.

Today is an exception. Her father is at work. And her nani, who lives with them, started complaining of chest pains half an hour ago. Mum had to take her to the hospital, leaving Avni under the able watch of a pesky neighbourhood auntie.

It's now or in sixty days. It'll be painful either way. Now is better, she decides. All she needs is the neighbourhood auntie out of her room for five minutes.

'Auntie,' Avni says to the middle-aged woman sitting across from her, reading a gossip magazine. 'I'm hungry. Can you make me a bread omelette?'

The woman narrows her eyes. 'Your mother said you already had breakfast.'

'Yes, I did. I think it's the chemo. Gives me splitting headaches.' She massages her temple in pretence. 'The headache usually subsides if I eat.'

The cancer excuse always works, she's realized. Tell people you want something because you have cancer, and they'll fulfil all your wishes with puppy-dog eyes.

'*Achcha, achcha. Theek hae.*' The woman drops the magazine on the side table, steps out of the bedroom and makes her way to the kitchen.

Avni jumps from the bed. She walks into the common bathroom that connects her room with her parents' bedroom. Like a cat, she tiptoes into her parents' bedroom to the secret hiding place. It's where she keeps love notes and trinkets from ex-boyfriends, away from the prying eyes of her parents. It's her collection of memories, from a time before cancer ravaged her life. Her nosy mother does monthly checks of Avni's room—her closet, under the mattress, her bookshelf, her college backpack. The one place she doesn't check is her own room. It's risky, but it's the perfect hiding place.

Avni waits. When she hears auntie whisk eggs in the kitchen, slowly, with nimble hands, Avni opens her mother's wardrobe. The door creaks open. Avni stands still, listening. The whisking continues unabated from the kitchen. Satisfied, she bends down and from the bottom shelf, where her mother keeps old handbags—junk that she doesn't use anymore but doesn't want to throw away—Avni pulls out a black, unbranded satchel that is moulding around the edges. Her stash.

Avni unzips the satchel.

'Avni!' auntie calls out.

Shit!

'You want any vegetables in your omelette?' auntie shouts from the kitchen.

Avni dashes to the bathroom, satchel in hand, and shouts back, 'No, auntie!'

She hears footsteps coming towards her. The footsteps stop outside the bathroom, in her parents' bedroom. 'Are you in the bathroom?'

'*Hanji*, auntie,' she says in a low, sick voice.

'Everything okay?'

'I'm queasy. That's all.'

'I'll stand here while you finish up.'

'It's okay, auntie.'

'No, no. Your mother told me not to leave you alone.'

Shit! Avni closes her eyes. She is sweating, her palms moist against the leather satchel.

Suddenly, it dawns on her. She has everything she needs. Right here in the satchel, in the privacy of the bathroom.

She rummages inside the satchel and pulls out a syringe-needle pair. She'd tricked the nurse and stolen it during her last hospital visit. It's a 10 ml syringe, 21-gauge needle—much smaller than the 20 ml syringe, gauge-7 needle that the Dreamcatcher had sent in the *Dream Box*. She's researched online and done the math.

'Oh, your mother left her wardrobe door open,' says auntie. 'Let me shut it.'

Avni doesn't have time. She unwraps and attaches the needle to the syringe. She pulls the plunger, filling the syringe with air.

She swallows hard. It'll hurt. *But no going back now.*

Avni moves closer to the bathroom mirror. Lines up the needle against the jugular in her neck.

Avni gulps and thrusts the needle inside her neck. She squirms as the needle pricks and breaks through the skin. She pushes the plunger, filling the air into her bloodstream.

Nothing happens.

She pulls the needle out. Fills the syringe with air. Pushes it back in.

Nothing happens.

She does it again. And again.

Her hands start trembling. Soon, the shivers turn into palpitations. Unbearable pain courses through her chest.

Her vision blurs. She can't breathe. Her feet falter, her hands grab the bathroom sink.

'Avni, everything okay?' auntie asks.

In the mirror, she sees auntie open the door, slowly.

No!

Avni twists around. In one swift motion, she pushes the door shut and bolts it.

'Avni, open the door!'

Avni isn't listening. She stumbles to the other door, breathless. She bolts it shut with the last remaining ounce of energy.

Avni slips and crashes to the bathroom floor, her head banging against the toilet seat.

'Avni!' Auntie bangs the door. 'Avni!'

Her head throbs, her chest burns, and her heartbeat slows down.

'Fuck you, cancer . . .' she says with her last breath.

37

 Audio Journal of *THE DREAMCATCHER*
Audio File #9

I am a pathological liar. I can't help it. It comes so naturally to me. Kids grow up learning that honesty is the best policy. I learned early in life that it isn't. Sometimes I do it just to see if I can get away with it. It's like a game. A challenge. And I'm good at it.

I was eight. Mom had asked me to get bread from the neighbourhood *kirana* store. I pilfered a lollipop while no one was looking. I came back home, and mom asked me about the lollipop. Because it was in my mouth! I was *that* stupid. Instead of hiding and eating it later, I couldn't wait to pop it into my mouth. Okay, I was eight, but still! So, mom asked me, and you know what I said? I started crying and admitted I had filched it. Mom sat me down and gave me a lesson I'd never forget. She said, if you are going to lie, think it through. Think of every scenario, think of every question, think of every counterargument. She gave me ten minutes and asked me to come up with three acceptable reasons why an unpaid-for lollipop was in my mouth. I was quite pleased with the ones I came up with:

1. The kirana store uncle gave me the lollipop for free.
2. I found the lollipop on the ground. I asked around. Nobody wanted it.
3. There was a discount on the bread. I bought the lollipop from the money saved.

Mom graded my answers. She showed me the loopholes; showed me where I'd get caught. Discount on bread? She'd know or she could easily check it with the kirana store uncle.

Guess which answer she found the best?

The second one.

Why? She thought I'd be scolded for picking up dirty things from the ground, but one couldn't be sure if I was lying. There were no witnesses, proofs or no way to cross-check with the kirana store owner.

I learned an important lesson that day: sometimes, it's best to admit a little to get away with a bigger lie.

38

Simone gulps down a glass of fresh orange juice. She has just returned from a morning ten-kilometre run, energized and spirited, sweaty and sticky.

Simone thumps down on a chair in the dining room and unfurls the morning newspaper. It is her moment to cool before she showers and heads to Tihar Jail. She has been volunteering at the prison for a week now. She has all the time in the world since she's still on suspension, and it gives her a chance to spend precious time with Shobha amma.

Simone unwraps a protein bar and takes a bite. She stops munching as a news headline grabs her attention.

TERMINALLY ILL TEEN COMMITS SUICIDE BY INTENTIONAL AIR EMBOLISM

Simone speed-reads the article. Her heart sinks. *Avni?* She knows the victim. She thought she'd saved Avni from the Dreamcatcher. But she was wrong.

Bile rises from her stomach. She is furious. She can't even do anything about it. They have forced her to stay at home. Suspended. 'Fuck!' she yells.

She picks up her phone and calls Lucas.

'Did you read the news about Avni?' she says when Lucas answers.

'I don't need to. I was at the crime scene in Guwahati yesterday. Flying back to Delhi in an hour.'

Of course! It's still their case. And Lucas is the lead detective now that Simone is on a timeout.

'Did the Dreamcatcher do it?'

'No, seems like an open-and-shut suicide. There was a neighbour in the house who witnessed it.'

Simone bites her lower lip. It still doesn't vindicate Dia, the Dreamcatcher. She planted the idea of suicide in Avni's mind.

'Did you go through the recording of the Dreamcatcher with Avni? The one we missed.'

'Yes, I did.' Lucas sounds exasperated. 'There is nothing there.'

'You sure?'

'Simone, forget discussing the case. I shouldn't even be talking to you.'

'But you are. So, tell me, are you sure?'

'Yes, I'm certain.'

'Then you wouldn't mind sending the recording to me?'

Lucas sighs aloud as if trapped. 'Okay, fine. I'll forward you the recording on WhatsApp. I can't send it to you on your official email. Keep it to yourself, will you?'

Simone grins. 'Of course,' she says and disconnects the call.

Within minutes, her phone dings. Lucas has shared the audio file with her. Simone grabs her earphones and plays it.

The audio starts with the Dreamcatcher asking Avni if she has lit the ketamine candle and stuck the Dreamo device on her forehead. Once Avni confirms, she asks her to relax, lie down on the bed, and place the syringe with a needle inserted next to her hand. What follows is a ten-minute guided meditation. It's eerily similar to the one Dia had used with Simone during her therapy session. *Is this how Dia hypnotizes?*

Simone clenches her hands into fists. It's another clue linking Dia to the murders, but it's circumstantial. *The court won't indict Dia based on guided meditation.*

There is a long silence on the audio. *Did it end?* Simone checks her phone. *No.* She fast-forwards the audio. Soon, Simone hears the soft, rhythmic snoring of Avni.

The Dreamcatcher starts narrating Avni's story in second person. And soon, it turns depressive when cancer, the villain, is introduced. Even hearing it on the recording touches a chord with Simone's stony heart. *It's the depth and command in the Dreamcatcher's voice.*

And suddenly, the Dreamcatcher stops mid-sentence. Simone hears urgent shuffling, and the line goes dead. Something else caught the Dreamcatcher's attention. Something urgent. *Like the police knocking on her door.*

Simone checks the timestamp. The entire video lasted fifteen minutes. It matches the time Simone took to reach

Dia's bungalow and haggle with the constable before he called Dia's assistant.

Simone replays the audio file. The guided meditation starts after the initial setup, then a prolonged silence—Simone fast-forwards it again—then the story narration, and then the abrupt ending.

Lucas was right. There is nothing untoward in the recording.

Simone sighs. Sits back in the chair. She is enervated. *What am I missing?*

Absent-mindedly, she presses the play button again, letting it play in the background while she wrestles with the puzzle, to piece it to form concrete evidence to pin Dia. She thinks over each step followed by the Dreamcatcher to select victims at the Dream Cancer Foundation, convince them that suicide is the right last resort, train them in lucid dreaming and finally, murder them in their sleep.

The guided meditation starts in the background.

In her mind, Simone goes through each clue, each piece of evidence they found at the murder sites. The Dreamos, the candle, the earphones—and now the guided meditation—that link Dia to the murders. But whichever way she cuts or slices the problem, the conclusion remains the same—it's circumstantial evidence. They have nothing to implicate Dia.

The guided mediation ends. A long silence ensues.

Simone looks up at the fan rotating above her head. Her mind wavers to Tihar Jail and the last few days with Shobha amma. How in a short time—

What was that?

Simone sits up straight. She heard something pop up in the audio recording, like a stray heart murmur on a flat line. She had fast-forwarded this bit the last two times.

Simone grabs her phone. Scrubs the audio file back by ten seconds. She presses play and listens intently.

There it is! It's a whisper. *Did the Dreamcatcher say something? No, this voice is soft.*

She rewinds and hears it again. No, she can't make out what is being said. She tries again. No luck.

Maybe it's just static. Maybe it's my brain forcing me to form a clue against Dia.

No, there is something. Even if it turns out to be nothing, she wants to find out what it is. And she knows just the person for the job.

Simone finds the number on her contact list and calls.

'Hello, this is voice coach Sid Reddy . . .'

Give it a break 'voice coach'.

'. . . how can I help you today, Simone?'

He has my phone number? And it dawns on Simone that she herself gave him the number.

'Sid, I need urgent help.'

'At your service, madame.'

'There is a background voice in an audio recording I have. Can you separate the voice and sharpen it so it's more audible?'

'Easy-peasy. Send me the file. Tell me the exact timestamp of the voice, and I'll let the software work its magic.'

'Doing it now.'

Simone disconnects the call and sends him the file. Within minutes, he replies—*here's the sharpened audio*—with an attachment.

Simone opens the file and listens, holding her breath.

'. . . *no . . . chai* . . .' She hears two words interspersed with silence.

No chai? What does it mean?

She plays it again. Despite the sharpening of the sound, the voice is muted, like someone whispering from inside a locked room. But it's clear that someone is talking to the Dreamcatcher in the background.

Maybe Lucas was right all along. The Dreamcatcher is more than one person.

39

Simone calls Lucas.

'Simone, I really don't have the time to discuss—'

'You were right, Lucas!'

Lucas pauses. 'About what?'

'The Dreamcatcher is not one person. It's two. At least. Maybe more.' Simone tells Lucas about the murmur in the audio file, a voice that says, '*no chai*'.

'No chai? Like you don't want tea? Or there is no tea? I don't understand what it means,' says Lucas.

'Neither do I.' Simone admits. 'I'm sending you the audio file. Have a listen.'

Simone receives a second call from an unknown number.

'Lucas, I'm getting another call. Talk later.' Simone disconnects and accepts the call from the unknown number.

'Hello. Is it CBI officer Simone Singh?' says a frightened, breathless voice.

'Yes, speaking.'

'Simone, ma'am, I need help. I didn't know who else to call.'

'Sorry, who is this?'

'Noor. Noor Shah. You saved me from the Dreamcatcher. I was there that day when you arrested Dia ma'am.'

'Yes, I remember you, Noor. How can I help?'

'You must save me, ma'am!'

'Save from whom?'

'She threatened me. She threatened to kill me. She coerced me to lie. But after reading about Avni in the newspaper today, I want to come clean. I will reveal everything.'

'Who threatened you?'

'Dia and . . . Radhika, her assistant.'

Simone sits up straight. This changes everything. Noor is a primary witness. Dia was saved only because of her testimony, a lie. And Radhika? Suddenly, it strikes Simone. *It was Radhika's voice on the audio recording. She was perhaps asking Dia for tea.*

Noor continues, her voice is patchy and croaking, as if on the verge of tears. 'And last night, someone entered my apartment and killed my cat while I was sleeping. I found Sambha with a knife plunged into his chest this morning.'

'Who's Sambha?'

'My cat. My dead cat.' Noor bursts into tears. 'I know they did it to scare me. To show me the consequences if I reveal the truth.'

'Where are you, Noor?'

'I just ran away, ma'am. I saw my dead cat and ran away from home. I'm scared, ma'am. I'm scared.' Noor pants and heaves.

'Noor, tell me where you are,' repeats Simone, raising her voice.

Noor sniffles. She hesitates.

'I will protect you, Noor. I promise.' Simone calms her voice down, realizing she is speaking to a teenager—a rich, pampered, and scared child. 'Tell me where you are, and I'll come get you.'

Noor breathes into the phone, deciding. 'I'm at Hotel Desire on G.B. Road. Room 201.'

'Stay there. Don't step out and don't accept any calls except mine,' says Simone, while rushing to grab her Jeep keys. 'I'm on my way.'

Simone disconnects the call.

40

Simone slams the brakes of her Mahindra Thar outside Hotel Desire, a three-story derelict structure in Delhi's red-light district—grey, no paint or whitewash, chipped and broken in patches. Despite broad daylight, a neon sign on the building flashes the hotel's name, switching between fluorescent green and sleazy pink.

Simone bolts to the front door and enters the narrow lobby. There are no security guards, no doorman. It seems like they converted a sordid apartment building into a makeshift hotel. The carpeted lobby reeks of the sweaty-sock odour of mould. A desk has been placed at the entrance to serve guests. A large sign on the desk reads: *Cash Only*. Behind the desk, on the wall, is pasted an A4 print-out of the hotel's TripAdvisor 'Certificate of Excellence' and customer rating—a five out of five!

The guests were clearly happy with the services, or the lack of them, while they went about their illicit business in private.

A bellboy sits behind the desk. He looks like a teenager, probably still in school, if he attends any. 'Welcome to

Hotel Desire. Your privacy is our priority. How can I help?' he says in a monotone, as if repeating a line committed to memory.

'Room 201?' asks Simone.

'First room on the second floor,' he says and points to a staircase in the far corner.

Simone dashes up the stairs, two at a time, to the second-floor landing. There are four rooms on either side of the stairs. Simone walks to room 201.

She knocks on the door, once.

No response. No sound.

She knocks again, harder, longer this time. Same response. Nothing.

Simone's phone rings. It's Noor.

'Ma'am, is it you outside my room door?' she sounds panicked.

'Yes, it's me. It's safe to open it.'

Almost immediately, the room door opens. 'Thank you for coming, ma'am!' says Noor, fidgeting on her feet.

Simone enters the narrow passageway and shuts the door behind her. Noor latches onto Simone in a manner in which the toddler clings to her mother.

Simone cringes, smelling Noor's dirty, sweaty hair. She is still in her pyjamas, her hair is astray, and her breath stinks. It seems Noor woke up, ran to the hotel from her apartment, and fell straight into a dustbin.

'I'm here now. Please let go of me,' says Simone.

Noor steps back. 'Sorry ma'am, I'm just relieved you are here. Please come in.'

Simone follows Noor. The passageway opens into a square room with a bed in the middle and a table-chair set in the far corner. Noor's large luggage bag is open on the table. It's filled with haphazardly packed clothes, accessories and footwear as if Noor dumped whatever she could find and ran for her life. Light dapples through the sheer drapes that sheath the window. The room smells of burnt plastic—probably cocaine—and latex, probably used condoms. What else can you expect from a hotel named Desire in the middle of the red-light district? thinks Simone

Noor pulls out the chair for Simone. 'Please take a seat, ma'am,' says Noor, her hands clasped together, back hunched and face tense.

'No time to waste. Pack your things. You are coming with me. You can stay at my house for the time being until your parents arrive from Mumbai. I'll make sure that they put you under police protection.' Noor is Simone's golden duck, the only witness who can incriminate Dia. She'll protect her with her life if needed.

Noor gulps and nods. 'I only unpacked a few clothes and toiletries. Shouldn't take long to pack them.'

'Be quick. I'll wait outside,' says Simone.

'No, ma'am! Please, can you stay here? I'll feel safer knowing you are here.'

Simone shrugs her shoulders. 'Okay, go on.'

Noor lets out a sigh of relief. She rushes to the cupboard and removes a few blouses and jeans from hangers. She pushes things around in the suitcase and dumps the clothes. Simone notices a photo frame in the bag. Noor's smiling at the camera, her tongue sticking out to one side, playful and coy. There's another person with an arm around Noor's neck, but a blouse is covering the rest of the photo frame. *Teenagers*, thinks Simone.

Noor rushes to the bathroom to collect her toiletries.

Curiosity takes the better of Simone. She bends down, pushes away the blouse, and sees the photo frame in complete view. There's another girl in the photo. Her arm around Noor. Her tongue is also sticking out, touching the edge of Noor's tongue. It's playful. It's romantic.

The face is familiar. She has seen the other girl before. *Where?*

Suddenly, it strikes her. It's Sonali, the Dreamcatcher's first victim. The first victim is usually the trigger for serial killers. She remembers what Sonali's mother said. Noor and Sonali were best friends. From the photo, it seems they were more than friends. Sonali's mother had held Noor responsible for her daughter's death. In fact, Noor was a suspect before . . .

Simone gasps, her mind churning. Noor was a suspect before she became a victim. They gave her a free chit only because she is a victim. Was it staged? Was it intentional?

Simone's mind darts back to the day she busted through the door of Noor's apartment to save her. Noor's master bedroom was engulfed in ketamine smoke. *But why were there so many candles burning when the Dreamcatcher only sent one candle in the Dream Box to each victim?*

And there was nobody else in the house. No person. No *cat*.

Noor rushes back from the bathroom and dumps toiletries in the suitcase.

'Noor,' says Simone. 'When did you buy a cat?'

'Cat?'

'Yeah . . . Sambha?'

'Ah! Many years ago. When Sambha was a kitten. Why?'

'We didn't find any cat when we saved you from the Dreamcatcher.'

'Umm . . . yeah, yeah, Sambha was with a neighbour that day.' Noor looks away and zips up an inside pocket in the suitcase.

Simone narrows her eyes. Another thought pops into her head. Noor lives in Gurugram. If she was so scared, why did she come all the way to central Delhi instead of a hotel in—

Simone feels the sudden, sharp piercing of a needle in her neck.

'Fuck!' she yells, slaps Noor's hand away, and jumps up from the chair, clutching her neck.

But it's too late. Noor has injected something inside her.

'What are you doing?' she asks, her feet unsteady, her head dizzy.

A cunning smirk graces Noor's face. She tilts her head to one side. 'Relax, Simone. It's only a sedative. You aren't dying. At least, not for now.'

Simone's knees buckle. She falls to the floor.

Noor bends down, her head close to Simone's. 'I heard you've been depressed lately?'

Simone wants to punch her in the mouth. She tries. Her hands don't acquiesce. Her body is numb.

'Let me help you, Simone. Let me guide you to end this miserable life of yours.'

Noor rummages in her pyjama pocket and takes out a device. It's Dreamo. She sticks it on Simone's forehead.

Noor tilts her head again, grinning. 'Simone, would you like a tour of dreamland with the Dreamcatcher?'

41

Lucas fiddles with the pen in his hand. He leans over the notepad on the airplane tray tab in front of him. A cup of coffee has gone cold. On top of the notepad, in bold, he has written two words with a question mark: NO CHAI?

He has spent the last two hours scribbling and doodling on the notepad, his mind calculating the many permutations and combinations of the two words. It still makes little sense.

He plays the audio recording again—probably for the hundredth time—on full volume. He presses the earphones deeper into his ears as if it'd help him hear better. The recording plays like it has played many times before. The soft, muted voice comes up on the audio. There is a distinct pause, small and quick, between the two words, he infers. '. . . *no, chai*? . . .' He adds a comma in-between the two words on the notepad. Someone is asking the Dreamcatcher a question.

You won't have tea? He repeats it in his head. But then, shouldn't it be — '*no chai*?' —without a comma, no pause.

There is a pause. It's unmistakable.

He plays the recording again. He closes his eyes so his brains fully attend to his ears. No change. The words remain the same.

Someone is asking if the Dreamcatcher will have tea. *It's like—'Lucas, chai?'. Lucas, will you have tea?*

'Cabin crew, please prepare for landing.' The captain's voice comes up on the Tannoy.

Lucas fidgets, knowing he'll have to put up the tray table soon. But he pulls back his thoughts to the problem at hand. *Is the first word a name?* The words are spoken quickly, but there is a distinct pause.

He replays the audio. His mind wanders. If Simone was right—and the tracer was to be believed—then it must be someone at Dia's bungalow. Who all were there that day? Dia, Radhika . . . *and Noor.*

'Noor, chai?' he mutters. He repeats, this time speeding through the name.

He gasps. It fits. Someone asked Noor if she'll have tea. *Is Noor the Dreamcatcher?*

42

 Audio Journal of *THE DREAMCATCHER*
Audio File #10

Sonali would come alive as she took control of her dreams. She'd laugh like a maniac. She'd curse with gusto. She'd smile as far as her lips could stretch. She'd become everything she had—and I had—lost in her life. The last stage of cancer had robbed her of who she was. Severe depression had blown away the spark that made Sonali, Sonali. So, lucid dreaming became our last refuge. Our nightly sojourn. Our happy place.

And it happened one night. Sonali was lucid dreaming while we were on a video call. I was guiding her dreams, hypnotizing her by suggestion, when she whispered, I want to touch your face,

Noor. She'd mumble often while lucid dreaming. So, I suggested she raise her hand and touch my face. I expected her to do it in the dream. But lo and behold! She actually raised her hand and reached out. While dreaming! It was crazy, bro! It felt like I had performed a magic trick without knowing how to.

I thought it was a fluke. So, I tried again. I told Sonali to imagine we were in a nightclub, dancing to the beats of *Jugnu* by Badshah. Then I asked her to raise both her hands and perform bhangra. She did! I was totally gobsmacked. It wasn't a fluke. I could make a lucid dreamer move their limbs. I could make them dance to my tunes, literally.

When Sonali woke up, I was so excited to tell her about what had transpired. I had hypnotized her, made her hands move over a call while she was lucid dreaming. I didn't think it was possible. But it was!

You know what was her first reaction when I told her? She said, 'Oh, perfect! Can you make me shoot myself in the head while lucid dreaming?'

43

I am on Mars, thinks Simone.

A red sandstorm, more grainy than sandy, leaps off jagged rocks in a distance, swirls, twirls, before charging at her with full speed, like a swarm of bees chasing after the human who stoked its hive.

Should I run? She should, but she remains rooted. A part of her wants to stay rooted and embrace the sandstorm. It's the part that wants to die. She wants the grains to pelt her naked limbs. She wants little fires burning her skin. But another part of her, smaller and scared, wants to run and escape the treacherous storm that is upon her.

'Help,' she whispers. But she can't even hear her own voice amid the whistling of unrelenting winds.

'Grab my hand, Simone!' A voice rumbles.

She looks around. There is no one.

The sandstorm gathers speed; charges at her.

'I'm here!' the voice says again.

'Where?' she shouts.

'Look up!' says the voice.

Simone looks skywards. A single colossal arm juts out from the sky, like the stretchy arm of Doctor Reed Richards from the Fantastic Four cartoons. There is no face, no torso, just an arm and a hand.

The specks of rusty dust ram against her skin. The sandstorm is upon her.

'Grab the hand!' the voice says again, more urgently now.

Simone jumps up and grabs the outstretched hand. It lifts her up, and the next moment she is flying in space, wallowing in the ocean of stars. Simone looks up at the giant hand holding her. And she suddenly realizes—it's her own hand! Her hand pulled her out of the sandstorm. How is it possible?

'Am I dreaming?' she murmurs to herself.

'Of course, you are dreaming, Simone,' says the voice in her head.

She heaves a sigh of relief.

'Who are you?' asks Simone.

'I'm you. Your hand, your guide.'

'Where are you taking me?'

'I'm not taking you anywhere. You are taking us. You are in control, Simone. It's your dream. You are the pilot. You control me.'

'I do?'

'Yes. Try pulling me up.'

She tries to lift her arm. It doesn't move.

'Try again,' says the voice. 'This time, concentrate with your mind. Focus. Ask the mind to pull me—your arm—up.'

Simone focuses the mind on her arm. Nothing happens. She sighs.

'Stay focused. It's your mind. Make it listen to you. It'll do your bidding. Ask it—no, order it—to lift your arm.'

She focuses harder. She concentrates longer. And suddenly, the arm lifts itself. They are flying higher, faster.

'You did it, Simone!' says the voice in her head.

She laughs. 'Yes, I did!'

'What would you like to do next? Where would you like to go?'

She mulls it over.

'How about we visit your mother at Tihar Jail?' suggests the voice.

For some reason, her mouth waters, the taste of sweet halwa tingling at the edge of her tongue. 'Yes!' she answers.

The stars dissolve, space fades away, and the next moment she is at Tihar Jail, in the VIP visitor room, tapping her feet on the floor, waiting for Shobha amma, as she had on her first visit.

Her mother limps inside with a bowl of sooji halwa in her hand. She is smiling.

'Mother looks old. She is dying, isn't she?' says the voice in her head.

Suddenly, the smile washes away from Shobha amma's face. She looks frail, aged and scared. The scene was superimposed with another—a painting was painted over by someone. It was happy in one moment, downcast the next.

'Help!' says Shobha amma.

The limp in amma's leg becomes more pronounced. Her legs totter. Her arms flail. She falls.

'No!' screams Simone.

On instinct, she raises her arm and catches Shobha amma in her giant hand, right before she hits the stony floor. But the halwa splatters on the floor.

Simone starts bawling like a toddler.

'Shh! It's okay, Simo. Everything's okay. Stop crying.' Shobha amma embraces her, tries to calm her down.

The door flings open behind her. A man stands in the doorway, a burning cigarette tucked in-between his lips, a belt dangling from his hand, its silver buckle shining against the moonlight. Simone cannot make out the man's facial features. He's a silhouette, a shadow of someone she knows. *Who?*

'Dad?' The word sounds like a curse as it escapes her lips.

Dad wobbles on his feet and comes near her. 'Stop crying, Simone!' he shouts in her ears, his speech slurred. Simone's face contorts on smelling the acrid, stale odour of alcohol on his breath.

He peers at amma. 'She cries all day. Shut her up, Shobha,' he yells. 'We should have killed her in the womb! We should have killed her the moment we knew it was a girl. A boy wouldn't have wailed on non-stop!'

Simone's cries grow louder.

'Shut up, Simone!' Dad raises the belt and brings it down with full force. The buckle cracks against her forehead. She squeals in agony, grasping her head, howling like a rabid pup.

Dad removes the burning cigarette from his mouth and says, 'I kid you not, Simone. I will jam this in your mouth if you don't stop crying.'

Simone wants to speak up. She wants to fight back. But no words come to her mouth. Her body remains numb with fear. Her loud cries flow unabated.

'Nobody wants you, Simone.' A woman enters the room behind Dad.

Grandma?

'See, how miserable you've made everyone's life?' Grandma comes and stands next to dad. 'Do us a favour and kill yourself,' she says. 'Like you killed me.'

'I'm sorry, grandma. I didn't mean to hurt you.' Simone lets out a loud, unrestrained yelp.

'But you did! I didn't deserve to die. You did!'

Shobha amma comes and stands next to dad and grandma. 'They are right! You deserve to die, Simone.'

'Kill yourself,' says dad.

'Be gone,' says grandma.

Simone whimpers. *They are right*. She doesn't deserve to live. She killed grandma. Shobha amma gave her up for adoption because she was so miserable. Nobody cares about her. Nobody loves her. And why would they? She doesn't deserve it—neither love nor life.

Use the syringe, says the voice in her head. It's the same voice which had pulled her out from Mars and brought her here. The same voice that had taught her how to control her hand in this dream.

'Syringe?' she murmurs.

And suddenly, out of nowhere, a syringe appears in her giant hand.

Plunge it in your neck, says the voice. *Plunge it!*

Her knees give way. She falls to the ground. Tears flow down her cheeks. Her lower lip quivers unrepressed. Drool slips out of her mouth. Simone lifts her hand and lines up the syringe against her neck, ready to push the needle inside.

'Push it in,' says grandma.

'Kill yourself,' says dad.

'Die!' says Shobha amma.

'Push it in,' says the voice in her head.

'If that's what all of you want, so be it,' she whispers, words tumbling out incoherently while she cries.

She is about to plunge the needle into her neck when her eyes catch sight of the sooji halwa scattered on the floor. It reminds her of the first time she visited Shobha amma. She was a stranger, a killer, who had given her up for adoption as a child. But on knowing her and listening to her reasons, she understood her. She found her mother, who much to Simone's shock, was a victim of cruel domestic abuse. Simone found her happy place, the aftertaste of sooji halwa tingling in her mouth.

Shobha amma loves me. She doesn't want me to die.

Simone stares at the three figures towering over her, waiting for her to insert the needle into her neck. And she suddenly realizes. It's a dream. It's a reflection of her mind. She can change it.

'Push it, push it,' says the voice in her head.

She becomes aware of the voice which has been manipulating this dream. *The Dreamcatcher—Noor!*

Wake up, she tells her mind.

The dream world shudders.

Wake up, she orders her mind.

The dream world starts to break apart. Soon it vanishes.

Simone's eyes flutter open. Her vision is blurry.

'Do it, Simone. Push it in!' she hears the same voice whispering in her ear.

Simone feels the syringe in her hand, the prickle of the sharp needle against her neck.

'Do it!' says the voice.

Simone twists her head. It's Noor.

Noor's eyes bulge out in fear, colour drains from her face as if she has seen a ghost.

Adrenaline courses through Simone's arm, and on instinct, she jabs the needle with full force into Noor's forehead and pushes the plunger.

Noor's piercing scream is the last thing she remembers before she loses consciousness.

44

Simone stirs and groans. Loud, excited voices are rattling on non-stop next to her. She groans loudly, hoping the chattering would stop. It doesn't.

'Were you aware Simone was in that hotel?' She hears one person ask.

'No, sir. I followed the GPS location of Noor's phone. But if you ask me, Simone single-handedly caught Noor, the Dreamcatcher,' replies another person.

'I'm not asking you, Lucas. Simone had no business being there. She was on suspension.'

Her face twitches in annoyance, recognizing the voice of SP Vijesh Jaiswal. She opens her mouth to defend herself, but no words tumble out. She is parched, her throat clogged.

Simone tries to pry open her eyes. The effort is taxing. Her head swirls, dizzy in the aftereffects of whatever drug she has been given. *Who drugged me? Why?* The answers elude her, before suddenly, it all comes back—the visit to Hotel Desire, the realization that Noor is the Dreamcatcher, Noor jamming a needle in her throat, her crazy lucid dream that nearly ended in her death. As if on cue, a ripple of pain runs through Simone's head.

'We can ask her, sir. I'm sure there is a valid reason,' says Lucas.

Simone's eyes flutter open, her groans grow louder. Finally, she fully opens her eyes to the cotton-coloured ceiling with twin-tube lights showering ivory light, salt-coloured walls and two porcelain-like plastic chairs that sit next to the bed. In between the chairs is a tiny table. A demure bouquet of yellow roses stands on it. SP Jaiswal and Lucas occupy both chairs.

'Oh, she is awake, sir.'

SP Jaiswal stands up and inches closer to Simone. 'How are you doing, Simone?' he asks.

She tilts her head, blinks a few times, and clears her throat. 'Can't complain . . . I have tried, but nobody listens.' Her lips twitch and smile.

SP Jaiswal chortles. 'Ha! I see the drug gave you a sense of humour.'

Simone tries to push herself up with her hands.

'Take it easy,' says Lucas, and helps her prop up in bed.

SP Jaiswal fills a glass with water and hands it to Simone. 'I'm sorry to bring this up now, but I need some answers, Simone.'

Simone nods, guzzles down the glass of water, and says, 'Sure.'

'Why were you at the hotel?'

'I received a distress call from Noor saying she is being threatened by Dia and her assistant Radhika. She confessed that she had lied earlier. Told me she had proof against Dia.'

'Did you call Lucas or the local police?'

'No.' Simone bites her lips. 'Noor was desperate. She needed urgent help. There was no time. I rushed to help.'

SP Jaiswal peers at Lucas and shakes his head.

'Then what happened?' asks Lucas.

'Noor was a mess when I reached the hotel. I told her to pack. Trust me, I intended to hand her over to the local police and put her under witness protection.'

SP Jaiswal isn't moved. It's clear he cannot yet trust Simone. 'Then?' he asks.

'While Noor was packing, I saw a few things in her bag, which alarmed me. It got me thinking, and I realized she'd lied. Before I could confront her, she injected me with some drug, confessed that she was the Dreamcatcher, and started to hypnotize me in my dream—the worst nightmare I've ever had because I remember it so vividly. And right when I was about to kill myself, I remember waking up from the dream for a split second and jamming the needle into her head instead of mine. That's the last thing I remember.'

Silence.

'Where is she?' asks Simone.

SP Jaiswal and Lucas exchange glances.

'Noor is in a coma,' says Lucas. 'The air bubble formed a blood clot in her brain. The doctors aren't sure if she'll wake up at all.'

'Well,' says SP Jaiswal. 'The way I see it, you caught the Dreamcatcher. She is incapable of hurting or killing more cancer patients. Case closed.'

'Not yet,' says Simone. A renewed resolve runs down her spine.

'What do you mean?'

'I think Noor had help from someone.'

'Do you have any proof?'

Simone bites her lower lip. All she has is a voice on tape asking Noor if she'll have tea. It could be Dia. It could be Radhika. Come to think of it, it could be anybody. They can't be sure. And even if they identify the voice, it doesn't prove that that person aided and abetted in the murders.

Simone isn't ready to give up. 'I just need more time to gather evidence.'

SP Jaiswal shakes his head. 'I can't allow you to run amok with this. We have found the serial killer. Case is closed. Job well done. Lucas will get a commendation and you—' He stares at Simone. '—will get your job back.'

Simone sits up straight. 'Sir, allow us a month. If we don't find incriminating evidence within this span, I promise I'll drop the case.'

SP Jaiswal says, 'I have made myself abundantly clear, Simone. The case is closed. I'm giving you a way back into the CBI. Take it.'

'But sir—'

'No, Simone.' SP Jaiswal moves closer and hisses. 'You have nabbed the Dreamcatcher. You'll be recognized for your bravery. Now, your choice is simple. Accept the reality and take your job back. Or deny it and you'll never be a police officer again.'

Silence. Simone is dumbstruck. She doesn't want a medal or recognition. She wants to bring justice to everyone who deserves it, not just the one who pulled the trigger.

'Your choice,' says SP Jaiswal. 'Either way, this case is closed.'

45

Dia enters Max Super Specialty Hospital in Patparganj, Delhi. She scrunches her nose as soon as she inhales the caustic smell of antiseptic. She adjusts the pleats of her saree. Today, she has chosen a simple white silk saree with a golden border, a matching blouse, understated slip-on footwear, a brown leather Gucci tote and no jewellery. It's a solemn occasion, and she dressed for it. Trust, she believes, takes root in the smallest specks of appearance. We believe what we see. Trust, then, is truly a perception of reality, right or wrong. Manipulate it the right way and the world kisses your feet. Celebrities and cult leaders know it, and the select few, like Dia, are naturally capable of reigning over the naïve and the uninformed.

Dia smiles at the thought, her chest inflating, fuelled by the enormity of the political ambitions she harbours. For now, she's happy to remain under the shadow of her father. But her father is getting old. He needs a political heir. The ruling party needs a political heir. At the right time, at the right place, she will play the right cards. For now, she must wait.

Dia walks to the elevator brimming with confidence and elan, the pallu of her saree snaking in her wake. The elevator takes her to the third floor. She knows the way. She visited this place a month ago when Noor was first brought here. Her patient, her student, rendered a vegetable. Dia is here on the insistence of Noor's mother, to help her decide if she must pull the plug on Noor's life support. They've waited a month. Noor's condition remains unchanged. The doctors have declared her 'brain dead', but Noor's mother clings on to hope. It's time to let Noor go, thinks Dia.

The elevator dings. Dia steps out, walks into Noor's room, and knocks on the door. A feeble voice asks her to enter.

Noor's mother is alone in the lavish VIP room, her expression sombre, her eyes puffy. She rises from the sofa and joins her hands in greeting—her movements are slow and strained. 'Namaste, Dr Sengupta. Please come in.'

Dia walks in. 'Namaste. Mrs Shah.' She takes the woman's joined hands in her own and squeezes them a little. She feels her facial muscles twitch. 'I'm so sorry. I can't imagine how much it must pain you to be asked to pull your own child off life support.' There's an audible catch in her throat. Her lips tremble.

Mrs Shah purses her lips. Her eyes become ruddy and tears well up. 'The doctor says it's time. But Noor is right here. She's still breathing. How can I let her go?' She points to the bed, where Noor lays sprawled, her eyes shut, unmoving, except for her heaving chest. A tube is connected to her mouth, a needle plunged into the back of her hand. A heart monitor shows normal blood pressure, the pulse is regular. It seems like Noor is taking a nap.

Mrs Shah says, 'You mentioned on the phone that there is a way to revive Noor. A last resort measure. Some sort of hypnotherapy to jump-start the brain?'

Dia bobs her head. 'Yes, I wanted to make sure that we try everything, absolutely everything before we give up on Noor.'

Mrs Shah nods along.

Dia continues. 'Noor's mind is still working. It's awake. It's functioning. I believe I can hypnotize it, cajole it to reset itself, like rebooting a computer.'

Dia exhales.

'I don't want to give you false hope,' she explains. 'The probability of success is low. But we must try.'

'I trust you, Dr Sengupta. You helped Noor when she was at her absolute lowest, hounded by depression. You pulled her out of it. You gave her hope. You gave her life back. If there is anyone who can help her now, it's you.' Mrs Shah pauses, and looks away. 'And besides, what other choice do I have? If you fail, I . . .' Mrs Shah bursts into tears, words unsaid but understood.

Dia touches her on the shoulders. 'Have faith. It may work.'

In between sobs, Mrs Shah says, 'And . . . it may . . . not.'

Dia nods. 'I need to be alone with Noor for the hypnosis. Would you mind stepping outside for ten to fifteen minutes? Maybe get yourself a cup of tea?'

'Sure, sure.' Mrs Shah wipes away tears, glances at Noor once, and hurries out of the room, closing the door behind her.

Dia smiles. Sometimes, it surprises her how easily she gets her way. She walks closer to Noor and sits on the edge of the bed.

'How are you doing, Noor?'

No response.

Dia leans in closer, her face inches from Noor's, and whispers, 'Sweetheart, I know you are in there, somewhere, listening to me. It's time to wake up.'

Noor remains still.

'I'm sorry it turned out this way. I was certain you'd remove the only thorn in our path—Simone. She was getting too close for comfort. Little did I know that my therapy would give her the mental strength to counter a talented hypnotist like you. I should have foreseen it.' Dia hangs her head and sighs. 'I should have been there with you. I could have saved you.' Her voice drops.

Silence.

Suddenly, Dia laughs a throaty, hearty guffaw. 'We both know that's a lie. I couldn't be seen at the crime scene. Where would I find deniability then? Imagine the news headline, 'Cabinet Minister's daughter, a murderer!' The risk was too high. And I had you, my trusted protégé. Why would I play with red paint wearing a white saree?' Dia smiles and then shrugs her shoulders. 'But it is what it is.'

She takes Noor's right hand in her own. 'We had a good run, didn't we?' Dia sits back and chuckles. 'Don't you think it's ironic that we find ourselves at the same crossroads as our depressed cancer patients? Battling the moral question: to support a wretched, unliveable life or to euthanize it?' She pauses. 'I know what you would have chosen for yourself. Euthanasia.'

Suddenly, Dia feels Noor's fingers twitch in her hands.

Dia drops Noor's hand and jumps up, astonished. 'Can you hear me, Noor?'

Noor's finger jerks up and down as if Noor is responding to the question. The rest of her body remains still, her face emotionless.

'You can hear me. Good, good.' Dia holds Noor's hand again and squeezes it. 'I'm going to save you, Noor.' She feels the tickle from Noor's roving finger in her palm.

Dia came here certain that Noor would be pulled off life support. No Noor, case closed. Father had brokered the deal with the inspector general of CBI. No more harassment without proof. With Noor dead, Dia would be off the hook. The police have no evidence linking her to the murders. Why would they? Noor was indeed the Dreamcatcher. All Dia did was nudge a little, teach a little and maybe brainwash a little.

'Isn't it freezing in here?' says Dia.

No response.

Dia stands up, still holding Noor's hand, and says, 'Let me pull up your quilt.'

She pulls up the quilt and gently pushes Noor's hand inside, hiding it from view. Noor's fingers fidget in her palms, as if struggling, screaming for help.

Dia tilts her head, gapes at Noor's unmoving face, and smiles condescendingly. 'Don't worry, Noor. I will help you. I will help convince your mom . . . to euthanize you.'

Dia peers at Noor's hand covered by the quilt. She can't see the fingers moving. Perfect!

'I think we should call your mother in and end her agony.'

Dia twists on her heels and walks to the door. She halts. 'I almost forgot,' she says, looking back at Noor. 'I had your apartment searched. And you'd be glad to know that I found the one piece of evidence against me—' Dia unzips her tote and retrieves a voice recorder. '—your audio journal.'

No response.

'You shouldn't have told me about its existence.' Dia flashes a forced smile. 'I enjoyed listening to your journal, especially this last entry.' Dia pushes a button on the device and the Dreamcatcher's voice—a rich masculine baritone—comes on.

'. . . I can't take credit for it all. It was a team effort! I was the Dreamcatcher—the lead actor, the doer, the hands and the legs. And Dia, the mastermind, the teacher. We were driven by a common purpose, a shared goal—to euthanize depressed cancer patients who wanted it, who deserved it. We ended their suffering. We brought them peace. It was a charitable act. Would I do it again? Hell yeah!'

Dia switched off the recorder.

'You know what you did there, Noor? You implicated me, you slimy little bitch! But fortunately for me, I found it before the police did.'

Noor doesn't respond or move.

Dia puts the audio recorder back into her Gucci tote.

'Goodbye, Noor. We had quite a journey saving lives, assisting cancer patients who needed us. I'm sorry it's the end of the road for you.'

Dia pauses before saying, 'But it's not the end of our mission. I have plans for the Dreamcatcher. I think I'll create another Dreamcatcher like I created you. What do you think?'

EPILOGUE

'There she is!' murmurs Lucas from the passenger seat next to Simone.

Simone swivels her head and watches Dia step out of the hospital entrance. She grips the steering wheel of the van as if it was Dia's neck.

'Huh,' sighs Lucas. 'Do you think it's weird that I still find Dia attractive?'

Simone forces herself not to roll her eyes. She continues to stare at Dia.

'She has a natural charm, a never-before-seen charisma, don't you think?' says Lucas.

'I think Dia is somehow culpable. Noor might have been the Dreamcatcher, but she had help. We traced that call to Dia's bungalow. I am certain Dia had a role to play in the murder-suicides. What role? We must find out without SP Jaiswal knowing that we are still investigating her, while we work on other cases.'

She watches Dia descend the steps at the entrance to the waiting Toyota Fortuner, a government-issued car for the family of the cabinet minister. Dia looks around while the chauffeur opens the car door.

Her eyes meet Simone's.

Dia flashes a broad smile at Simone. She says something to the chauffeur and strides over to where Simone and Lucas are parked.

'Hello, Simone,' says Dia. Then she turns to Lucas. 'And, hi, Lucas. I hope you aren't stalking me,' she says in a voice that is both seductive and spirited.

Lucas blushes, looks away and blurts, 'No, no. We are here in connection with another case.'

Dia turns her attention to Simone. 'It's good to see you back on active duty.'

'Guess I have you to thank,' says Simone.

Dia had signed off on Simone's sound mental health—a precondition to rescind her suspension. Simone doesn't know the details, but she believes it resulted from a handshake deal between the CBI brass and Dia's father.

'The pleasure was all mine.' Dia bows slightly. 'Though remember your monthly check-ins,' she warns.

Simone grits her teeth. They had revoked her suspension on one condition—monthly therapy sessions with Dia. Simone had accepted the compromise. She needs to be on active police duty to catch and bell the evasive cat, Dia.

Simone narrows her eyes. 'I'll be there.'

'Brilliant! I look forward to seeing you again, Simone.'

'Same here, doc. Same here.'

Simone Singh will be back . . .

Scan QR code to access the
Penguin Random House India website